spLit-LEVELs

a novel

Thomas Rayfiel

Simon & Schuster

New York

London

Toronto

Sydney

Tokyo

Singapore

SIMON & SCHUSTER
Rockefeller Center
1230 Avenue of the Americas
New York, New York 10020

A portion of this novel previously appeared in *The Quarterly*.

Designed by Songhee Kim
Manufactured in the United States of America

10   9   8   7   6   5   4   3   2   1

Library of Congress Cataloging-in-Publication Data
Rayfiel, Thomas, date.
    Split-levels : a novel / Thomas Rayfiel.
        p.   cm.
        1. Fathers and sons—United States—Fiction. 2. Suburban life—United States—Fiction. 3. Fathers—Death—Fiction.
I. Title.
PS3568.A9257S65   1994   93-33725
813'.54—dc20   CIP

ISBN 978-1-4391-8124-9

Claire

. . . frightened to discover he had remained practically unchanged since boyhood. Only his visions had increased in size, and he had overcome a number of the technical problems connected with them.

—Patrick White, *Riders in the Chariot*

spLit –
LEvELs

chapter 1

NOBODY WAS BORN HERE.
People came here, with children, to live in a lawnscape of
split-levels. Past the front door is cool tile, a twilit hall.
Steps lead up to the living room, down to the basement.
There are only closets and passageways here, then the
freezer, still surgically white and pure, with unknown
portions, the date frozen—but not the contents—written
with a special marker right onto the plastic:

7/4

12/26

4/15

Upstairs, a dictionary lies splayed on a lucite stand. The
carpet is synthetic, short stitches like the back of an em-
broidery or needlepoint. Below the picture window are
crystals and shells and a cactus. Books enfold one corner.
A globe lights up, faded papery world. Water has gotten

in under the continents. Above the brick fireplace, on hooks sunk into dark expensive panelling, is a section of Parthenon frieze in plaster. Head of a horse being reined in. It ends in a jagged, time-smoothed diagonal.

The house is mine now. I have come to take possession. But of what?

The last stairs lead to the bedrooms. They branch off from a central hallway. First mine, then my sister's. At the end of the hall is the door to my parents' room. Nothing has changed here. The huge green bed floats like a raft, something to shuffle around, one awkward sidestep at a time. A book is lying on the floor underneath the headboard. I stoop to pick it up, glimpsing dustballs. Thucydides' *Peloponnesian War*, long overdue from the municipal library.

The master bedroom has its own bath. A man is standing there with a gun. He points it level at my chest.

"That's evidence," he says.

"What is?"

"Everything." He nods to the book. "Everything here is evidence. How did you get in?"

"Key."

"I have all the keys."

"There's one behind the mailbox. For emergencies."

He frowns. He is a middle-aged black man in a suit and tie, gray at the tips of his mustache and the bottom of his sideburns.

"I'm the son," I explain, not moving.

"You are, huh? Allen Patrick Stanley?"

"Allen David Stanley."

He smiles, lowers the gun.

14

"That's right."

It's not a large bathroom. When he turns, his shoulders almost touch me. He directs my attention to the tub. It is crusted with a muddy brown powder.

"I'm Lieutenant Anderson," he remembers, holding out a hand. "We've been expecting you, Mr. Stanley. Down at the station, though. Not here."

"Why hasn't anyone cleaned up?" I ask, staring.

He shrugs.

"Not our job. We came in, took pictures, tried not to dirty anything. You can clean it off now, if you want."

"This is where it happened?"

"Yes."

I touch the thick lip of the tub. On some parts of the porcelain it has dried in a rusty streak. In other places it's more of a spray. The glaze is worn and porous. I can feel the baked clay. The tile floor bruises my knees.

"If you don't mind"—his voice has an echo to it—"there are some questions I'd like to ask."

"This is all?" I say, staring into the empty bath.

"All what?"

"All there is?"

"Well," he clears his throat. "What did you expect?"

"More."

"No," he says. "There's no more. This is it."

Downstairs, the furniture is still arranged to host an ideal, never-to-be-thrown cocktail party. I lift just slightly the leg of an end table, enough to see its years-deep mark bored into the carpet. Nothing has been moved. Lieutenant Anderson takes off his jacket. His leather shoulder holster, with its straps and buckle and gun, is like some obscene piece of lingerie. He is so thick and physical, in this house I thought inhabited only by ghosts.

"This key you mention," he starts. "The one behind the mailbox. That changes everything. We didn't know about that."

"How does it change things?"

"It raises the whole question of access."

He watches as I go to the liquor cabinet. I tilt the bottle toward him.

"No," he says. "But you go ahead."

"I was coming to the station," I say, sitting on the couch. "But I wanted to be here first. How did it happen?"

"Nobody knows. A neighbor saw mail piling up and called us. We knocked, then broke a window."

"Where is he?"

"In the county morgue." His eyes meet mine for a moment, then flick away. "Maybe I will join you."

He heaves himself out of his chair and makes himself at home, getting a glass from the cabinet, pouring. He's around forty-five, an ex-athlete, I decide, watching him go back and sit.

"Your father was in the tub," he finally says.

"How did he—?"

"Wrists."

There is a warm feeling in the pit of my stomach. It's the drink, unclenching muscles.

"The body wasn't discovered for several days." He holds his glass up to the light. "So it's very difficult to pinpoint the exact time. We like to do that, for the records. That's why I need to know when you last—"

I am watching my world, reflected in the slick of the whiskey, shake violently, an uncontrollable twitch in my elbow. Alcohol slops over the side and evaporates on my skin.

"Sorry." He comes over and takes the drink out of my hand. "I was thinking out loud. Bad habit. You should hear my wife on the subject."

"Did he leave anything?"

"No note. That's why I have to ask you these questions. He live alone?"

"Of course he lived alone."

"Your mother?"

"Dead."

"I'm sorry to hear that. When did you last speak to him?"

I want my drink back, but he's holding both now. I can't tell which is mine. He sees my dilemma and puts one glass down on the coffee table. Slowly, I raise it to my lips.

"I'm looking for any kind of reason," he says carefully, watching.

A bird thuds into the window, fooled by its own reflection, recovers and flies off.

"What did you want to know?"

"When you last spoke to him."

"I don't remember."

"A month? Two?"

"More than that."

"More! How come?"

Among the decorative objects on the picture window's

sill is a stone apple. Some mineral that mimics the red-yellow blush of the fruit. I squeeze it, the cold weight reassuring in my hand.

"Didn't get along?" he suggests.

"We got along fine. We didn't talk, that's all."

"So you couldn't tell me if he was depressed about anything?"

"I'm sorry, Detective, but—"

"Lieutenant. Don't have any detectives on our force. That's only in the movies. We're just a small suburban police department. Most of my work is in property damage. Vandalism and stuff. This is all new to me."

"Lieutenant, I was in the city this morning. I got a call. I came right out. I don't think I can help you."

"Haven't been home in a while, huh?"

"Years."

"Thirteen, isn't it?"

I look up.

"Who told you that?"

"People. And you're what? Around thirty? So you were just a kid when you left."

"I suppose."

"There was also a daughter, wasn't there? Your sister?"

"She's gone too."

"I'm sorry to hear that."

The whiskey is making my eyes water. I get up so my back is to him.

"You have anyone to call?" he asks.

"I'm fine."

"Family members who should be notified? Cousins?"

"No."

"Something about this . . ." he begins, troubled, then stops.

"What?"

"Never mind. Here's my number, if you need anything." He puts it on the table. "You *will* have to come down to the station. Give us an official statement. Think you can handle that?"

"I'll be there tomorrow."

"You go easy on that stuff."

I look down and see I'm holding a fresh drink.

Evening in the suburbs is artificial, like the light change in a stage play. You can never see the sun, just its increasingly oblique rays, flaying all substance from the abandoned toys, the cars, the clipped bushes, until everything is reduced to a facade. Stare long enough and the whole street loses its depth, becomes a painting. Then the lawn lamps go on. I put down my glass and drink from the bottle, try to sit by the window and watch. Around eight, the doorbell rings. There's no chain like in the city. And no way to look out. These houses were built in more trusting times. That was part of the appeal, their safety and openness. Windows large enough to crawl through, doors you could unlock with a paperclip. Now they scramble to graft alarm systems onto the original design.

"Hi!"

I still haven't turned on the porch light, so the figure is dark, a woman's delicate shoulders, with curly hair like clusters of grapes on either side of her invisible face.

She holds something in front of her with both hands, clutching it.

Fumbling inside, I finally find the switch.

"I'm your neighbor. Sally Bates. Remember me?"

She had been raking when I came in. A frank smile and a vague flat accent. Either the Midwest or the South. Some dying regional sound. Now I see her eyes are blue, her face weatherbeaten in places, but with an easy attractiveness to it. Her teeth are the whitest I have ever seen.

"I brought you dinner." She holds it out, a brown grocery bag. "I figured you hadn't had a chance to shop yet."

"Thank you."

I'm still holding the bottle and end up handing it to her. The bag is heavy and cold.

"I live right there." She points, reminding me. "We moved in about a year ago. My husband Bob, he teaches junior high. During the school year, that is. Now he's out at the Seven-Eleven. Graveyard shift."

"Would you like to come in?" I ask. "Have a drink?"

"Oh I couldn't." She peers a little way beyond the door, out of curiosity. "I found him, you know."

"Found him?"

"Your dad."

In the bag are two frozen TV dinners and a pint of ice cream.

"Maybe just for a minute," she goes on, brushing past me. "I'll watch you eat."

We sit at the kitchen table, a white Formica circle. She crosses her legs.

"You look like him," she smiles.

"Did you know my father?"

20

"Not really. Like I said, we just moved in a while ago. And your dad kept pretty much to himself."

"Everyone does here."

"That's the truth."

She's not forward, just starved for company, her husband out on the highway selling cigarettes and sixpacks. She wears jeans and a plaid cotton shirt.

"No kids?" I ask.

"Nope. Trying, though." She looks around the kitchen, cataloguing it, and takes a swig of liquor. "Yeah, I guess that's what people do here. Take care of their kids. They're all so inward. Not like where I come from."

"Where's that?"

"Kentucky. Met Bob in the army."

"You were in the army?"

"Military Intelligence. But I'm not supposed to talk about that." She finishes her drink and nods to the TV dinners. "Maybe I will join you."

Getting up, I catch a glimpse of her reflected in the oven's greasy glass door. She's rubbing the tops of her arms and shoulders, hugging herself as if she's freezing.

"How did you find him?" I ask, still turned.

"Well, the mail was all over. Newspapers, too. He got it delivered, you know."

"I know."

"So I called the police." She hands me the bottle. "Right off we could smell it. You're lucky. The place is really aired out now."

I don't usually drink this much. I have a cutoff point, very precise. But tonight it feels like I'm pouring the whiskey down a hole. Instead my surroundings are getting drunk, more significant and outlandish, while in the middle of it all I stay cold sober.

"I think you're supposed to peel back the cellophane on that cobbler."

The instructions are complex. My fingertips go numb gripping the edge of the package.

"That's for the microwave," she says, coming up and reading over my shoulder. "Here, let me."

The compartments of the TV dinner intrigue me, how neatly everything is separated. The tastes appeal to individual lusts, for salt, for fat, for sugar.

"When I first came here," she says, "I thought I could hang my laundry out, like we do at home. That's what a yard means to me. Then, when you put it up or take it down, you meet people."

"Instead, what do you do?"

"You're looking at it." She takes a last swig, tilting the bottle all the way back. The stretch of her throat goes down to where the top buttons of her shirt are undone. "You got any more?"

Together, we crouch in front of the liquor cabinet.

"This is just like back home," she drawls. Drunkenness thickens her accent. "Used to come down at night, after everyone was asleep, and go across the floor on my hands and knees so they wouldn't hear."

In back, we find a presentation decanter. A gift to my father from a colleague or old student, it's a ceramic jug in the shape of a grinning black slave boy. I run my hands over it, trying to find the cork, finally grasp the head and rip it off at the neck.

"Always drink the same drink all night long," Sally says approvingly. "That way you don't get hangovers."

We sit cross-legged on the living-room carpet, stare up at the wall prints, a series of catalogue-bought reproductions from the ancient world. Pompeii. The Goddess of Spring. Persephone Fleeing Hell.

"What about your dad? What did he do?"

"He was a professor." I watch a group of three naked women. The Furies. They are dancing in a circle.

"At the community college?"

"Classical history. He was retired, though."

"That must have been nice, having a dad who could tell you things."

"Things?"

"I mean history. Like how the world got started."

I smile.

"He did have a theory about that."

"Yeah?" She lies back on the floor, expecting me to go on. I stare at her pelvis, the jeans stretched flat across.

"Once upon a time," I begin, trying to remember, "we all worshipped the moon. The moon watched over all our lives. Its stages told us when to plant, when to harvest, everything. And women were the high priestesses of this moon religion. They called it the cult of the White Goddess."

"Sounds like a salad dressing," Sally murmurs, still on her back, hands behind her head. "White Goddess. You know, like Creamy Italian."

"The priestesses would eat leaves," I go on. "Ivy and laurel. Then they would hallucinate, go into frenzies and have visions. They would run through the forest and any man they came across they would either kill or have sex with."

"Premenstrual, huh?"

"What?"

"Sounds like they were all on the rag."

"Well, that's just it. They were. That's where the moon comes in. It all had to do with their cycle, which is . . . lunar. Every twenty-eight days. They were worshipping their own fertility. But they didn't know it. There was no link in their minds between sex and birth. So they didn't know what they were doing would lead to a child nine months later. Having a kid just seemed this act of incredible magic. It's what gave them their power."

"Kids?" Sally struggles to sit up again, interested.

"That's when it all changed." I find my father's words now. "When men made the connection between sex and birth. Then the gods became male. Because suddenly they realized what power they had. And all the myths of the ancient world are really about the new gods taking over, breaking up the ceremonies of the White Goddess. It's about how the sun took over from the moon. About how rationality took over from madness."

"Calm down," she says. "*That's* how the world began?"

"Well, the world we live in now."

"So your dad was a complete nutcake, huh?"

"No." I frown. "It was just a theory. He used to tell it to me at night, like a bedtime story."

"Bob says it could be radiation."

She is growing dim again, the way she first appeared outside the door. It's because the big picture window is

24

black now, night sucking out the room's weak lamplight. I should draw the curtain, but that would involve getting up. We pass the decanter carefully, hands gripping the slave boy's torso, meeting sometimes, touching, but mostly communing by matching each other drink for drink.

"What are you talking about, Sally?"

"Radiation. You know, from the basement. There's been all that stuff about it on TV. It makes you crazy."

"He wasn't crazy."

"Yeah? Then why'd he do it?"

"I don't know."

"You going to sell the place?"

"I suppose." I touch the carpet, paw it experimentally to see if it holds any sentimental value. "I did grow up here."

"That counts for a lot." It's hard to tell if she's being sarcastic or not. She doesn't seem to know herself. "You sit in one of these houses long enough, you begin to hear your heart beat."

I listen for it, my heart, or anything, the sound of traffic, the tick of a clock. But there's nothing.

"Well," she says, "I should go arrange myself in bed for Bob."

"Arrange yourself?"

"I like to be the picture of sleep when he comes in. My hair just right, a little makeup under the eyes, some blusher," she says drunkenly. "You wouldn't know about that, being a man. After all, I'm what he comes home to. And I love him."

We haul each other up. I see her to the door.

"What's your name?" she suddenly asks, panicking. "Hell, I've been doing all this talking and you've just been sitting there listening. You're tricky."

"My name is Allen."

"Allen," she tries out. It seems to agree with her. "Well, thanks for the drink, Allen."

"Thanks for dinner."

She weaves across the lawn, passes the invisible border onto her own property. I wait until her door opens and closes, then walk out myself. The heat has broken. The atmosphere is lush and cool. A cluster of trees stands before the perfectly trimmed edge where grass meets sidewalk. Across the street, our neighbors now have a dim, shadowy lawn ornament, a maiden with painted cement hair, holding out her hand. I lie down and clutch the grass, trying to get a purchase, something to anchor me through the choppy night. I hug the earth and hold on.

When we first came here, everything was new. Town had not grown outward from some center. In fact, "town" was the wrong word. We lived in a development, something that one day existed simultaneously over large adjacent tracts of land. The usual descriptions, how big, how old, its politics, its boundaries, did not apply, seemed borrowed and inappropriate. The street went nowhere, ended in mud and spilt nails. I played in piles of scrapwood, mounds of wet insulation. The trees were saplings, so short I could touch their tips. Each was braced with a rubber ring and supported by a cable pegged into the ground. At the edge of the development, past the last house, an abandoned bulldozer sat in the forest, slowly being swallowed by ferns. I would sit on its front seat, try pushing and pulling its rusted levers. It was the rubble, the torn fringe of the community that fascinated me. I felt I was an inch away from grasping it like the corner of a rug, peeling it back and discovering the stitched pattern underneath, the structure that made it exist.

Our house, too, had no history. We were the first to live here. Whatever family past we brought was lost in the sudden flood of space and light. My sister was fifteen. One day she took a bath and had me crouch in the next room, setting the arm of the record player back on the same song over and over. They were aiming for a synthesis those days. Lutes and electric guitars. Gongs in the echoplex. White bluesmen. I was ten, steam and sun seeping through the half-open door. Her hair was in a high turban of white towel. She raised her hand to let drops of water fall into the solid bar of yellow that lay across her legs.

"Don't look!"

I went back, lifted the needle, and tried setting it seamlessly into the groove. The song began again.

"Oh, I don't care," she decided. "You can come in if you want."

Our parents had gone away. They would be back tomorrow, she assured me. They were paying her fifty cents an hour and had left more, much more, hidden in the belly of the vacuum cleaner. For emergencies.

"Bring me the scissors," she called, realizing I hadn't moved. I banged up against the walls of the hallway, on purpose, to feel my body, and came back holding the sharp pair of sewing scissors the way I'd been taught, the point buried deep in my fist.

"Well come on."

Her shoulder blades, white and frail, stuck out as she hunched away from me. She held the towel to her chest now. Her hair was long and damp, faintly springy.

"The comb's by the sink."

Water welled and streaked the foggy mirror there. On tiptoe I nosed through the bars of reflection to see myself.

"Hurry up," she said. "Before I get cold."

"I'm all sticky."

"That's from the steam. Be careful."

I got down on the floor. The tiles bruised my knees. As I ran the comb against her scalp, her head would get caught by a tangle and jerk back.

"Ow!"

"Why do we have to do this?" I complained, freeing the teeth again. They travelled further each time.

"Because," she answered, still young enough to use that ultimate explanation. "OK, that's enough. You can go now."

"The song!" I cried, jumping up, not wanting to let it end.

"Never mind," she called again.

I reached the record player just in time to lift the arm. I heard the door to the bathroom shut, the lock click.

A car slows in front of the house. I am still outside, lying on the grass. Its headlights are almost invisible in the dawn, so weak I can see the filaments in each bulb. A swampy chemical smell blows down the street. Looking across, I see only washed-out green, the lawn ornament I imagined now gone. The car turns into the next driveway and a man gets out. Bob Bates, Sally's husband. He has a baby face with chubby red cheeks and black hair. He's shockingly short, maybe five three. I watch him stretch and look up at a window. He must be contemplating his wife, who has arranged herself in bed for him, hair spread evenly against the pillow, face made up to conceal a night of sleeplessness and drinking.

He opens the garage door and drives in.

chapter 2

THE WORLD SHAKES. THE earth opens. I blink in the sun and our old lawn mower appears, its engine crackling and spitting blue smoke. A teenage boy holds the black plastic handles. He has a wide chest, a crude handsome face, and shaggy blond hair. It's hard for me to tell, just emerging from a dream, if he's making the lawn mower go or if the machine is energizing him, they both seem so primitive and powerful.

"Who are you?" I ask challengingly.

But the mower is too loud. I can't even hear my own words. When he answers, his mouth just moves in a silent twitch. A superb physical specimen, the phrase itself, runs through my mind. The sleeves of his shirt and the legs of his pants have been ripped or scissored off. Threads still hang. It gives the impression he shot up overnight, burst through all his clothes and strode over here to mow the lawn. But why?

spLit-LEvELs

"Turn it down!" I finally scream.

He flicks a switch. We both wait until the engine chokes on its own fumes, sputters once, and dies. There's a moment of blissful silence before birds and the simple breath of day resumes.

"I'm George," he says. "I mow the lawn."

His hand, when I shake it, still bears the trembling motion of the machine. He is already more than half done. Methodical up-and-down rows. Where he's come to a tree or any other natural obstacle he has simply lifted the machine and resumed on the other side.

"I figured I'd keep doing it," he says. "It would look bad if I didn't. Especially in the summer. It really grows, the grass."

"How much did he pay you?" I ask.

"Ten dollars."

It's strange, waking up fully clothed. The bills in my pocket are a green mash. I pry some off a central chunk.

"Why didn't you wake me when you got here?"

"Didn't see you," he says. "I only look straight ahead. What are you, a detective or something?"

"I'm Mr. Stanley's son."

"Son?" His thick lower lip sticks out in disbelief.

"He didn't tell you about me?"

"Tell me what?"

"Nothing. I mean, he didn't mention my name?"

"No."

"Well, I'm Allen Stanley."

"George." He holds out his hand again, then remembers we already shook, and stops.

"Did you know my father well, George?"

32

"I guess. I mean, I mowed here every week."

"Did you talk?"

"Sometimes. He'd wave to me from the window. Then he'd come out when I was finished. We'd talk while I cleaned the blades and stuff."

"Talk about what?"

"Nothing. School. He wanted to know what I was reading there, things like that. Then this year he bugged me about what I was going to do after graduation." He looks up to the picture window, as if expecting to continue the exchange.

"Did he ever say anything about himself?"

George frowns. "What do you mean?"

"The last few times you mowed, did he act unusual or—?"

"Your dad was a great guy," he interrupts. "He talked to me like I was a real person. All that shit people said about him. I hated that."

I nod at the clattering leaves, the spotless blue sky. He looks at me with fascination.

"You grew up here?" he asks.

"Did he say anything, George?"

"You mean like why he was going to do it? No." He shrugs. "The last few times I didn't even see him."

"What do you mean?"

"He wasn't here. I did the lawn anyway. Like today."

"But how did you get the mower?"

"I have a key."

"To the house?"

"No, to the garage."

"But you can get into the house through the garage."

33

"I guess." He fiddles with the choke, adjusting it.

"What are you doing now?" I ask dully, watching his bleached blond head. It's the size of a basketball. "Now that you've graduated."

"Nothing," he answers, not looking up. "Living at home."

I nod to the mower, its rubberized pullcord.

"That used to be my job. But I could never get that thing to start."

"Yeah? It's easy."

He kneels and demonstrates, starts it with one enormous roar. Then the machine again seems to take control. He goes back to work, head low, almost level with his bulging biceps. He's like a farmer plowing, taking slow, measured steps.

Lieutenant Anderson has a partner, Wertz, a scowling man with dirty blond hair and a square jaw. Are all policemen ex-football players, I wonder, sitting in the small office they share, noting the framed picture he has on his desk. Not the wife and kids but twenty-two beef-necked adolescents, the bottom row kneeling, holding a sign that reads MARAUDERS.

"Pardon me for living," he asks, "but what else did you touch?"

"I touched everything," I say.

"It's a crime scene."

"What crime?"

"It's the scene of a police investigation."

"It's my house. There was no sticker on the door saying KEEP OUT."

"We don't have one of those," Anderson sighs. He's embarrassed by his partner. "You want to go over it one more time?"

For all his talk of making an official statement, no one is taking notes or even recording me. We just sit in a glassed-in cubicle, like the office to a small business.

"I didn't know if he was depressed or not," I repeat, unintentionally singsong. "I hadn't talked to him in a while."

"Why not?"

"We didn't have that much to say."

Wertz looks up.

"He was your dad."

I shrug.

"You're right about one thing." He shoves some stapled papers. "He wasn't sick. Autopsy shows no progressive diseases. Just natural aging. Maybe the guy was a bit hard in the arteries, but no cancer, no heart condition. What I want to know is, why aren't you crying?"

"You must excuse Sergeant Wertz." Anderson stares him down.

"Yes, excuse the sergeant," Wertz mimics. His own voice is angry, whiny. Anderson's is deep, like it came out of a radio.

"Your father's financial situation seems all right," Anderson goes on. "He had his pension. Social Security. The mortgage was paid off."

"That's a nice piece of change," Wertz offers. "Once you sell the place."

"Maybe I won't sell," I say. "Maybe I'll stay here."

They both look up.

"And do what?" Anderson asks.

spLit-LEVELs

The phone rings and he is called to the outer office. Wertz and I are left alone. He doesn't talk. I have brought the Thucydides I found under the bed. The library is one building over. I have been clutching it during the interview.

"You know," Wertz starts, "I was born here too."

"I wasn't born here. We came here."

"Yeah? How old were you?"

"Young," I admit.

"Harley's not from here," Wertz grins.

"Harley?"

He nods to Anderson's desk.

"So?" I ask.

"So he doesn't know."

"Know what?"

"About your dad."

"That's in the past."

"Sure it is." He leans back in his chair and sticks the soles of two worn shoes in my face. One has a petrified blob of gum pressed into it. "I remember you from school, don't I? You were a shy kid. Always had your nose in a book." He waits. "You remember me?"

"No." He seems hurt. I look at the photo. "I remember the football team."

He smiles.

"Of course you do. We were undefeated senior year. How could you forget?"

"I remember there was a boy with long hair. The first in the school. And a bunch of you held him down and hacked it all off with a razor blade."

He is drumming the desk with a pencil, doesn't skip a

36

beat. In fact, there is a dreamy smile on his face.

"Those were the days, huh?" he sighs.

"Can I go now?"

"Don't be silly."

Anderson comes back in.

"Just got off the phone with the Medical Examiner." He and Wertz trade a look. "We haven't been entirely straight with you."

"What do you mean?"

He frowns, still standing in the doorway.

"Well, there are these marks."

"Marks?"

"Marks on your father's arms. Bruises, above the wrists."

"There's five on each," Wertz adds helpfully. "Four fingers and a thumb."

"I don't understand."

"It's possible he was held," Anderson says.

"Held down." Wertz demonstrates, coming around the desk, clamping my own forearm in his hand. "One at a time, see? Hold it with one, cut with the other. He was an old man. It wouldn't have been hard. Hell, I could do it to you."

His fingers press, then release, leaving a set of red marks where the blood rushes back in.

"It's a possibility," Anderson says. "Other things are funny too."

"Funny?"

"No blade," he offers. "We can't find it anywhere. A man kills himself, he doesn't go hiding the razor blade he uses."

37

"It fell somewhere."

"We searched extensively."

I try visualizing the bathroom. Except for the bloody tub, all its surfaces are bare and pure.

"The bruises were recent," Anderson goes on. "Probably coincident with the crime."

"Crime?"

"Homicide," he says precisely. "I didn't think you were capable of handling it when I first met you. I'm not sure you're capable of handling it now. But the medical evidence strongly suggests—"

"Murder?" I say. "You can't be serious."

"Take a look."

It all seems choreographed, rehearsed, the way they keep drawing my attention, first Anderson, now Wertz. Back and forth. Wertz lays the eight-by-ten photos in front of me. They look for a moment like abstract patterns, senseless angles and clouds. Then they are my father. An old man's face, still boyish though, the wasted grin, the flowing white hair, his straight nose and sharp jaw. A profile reduced to simple lines. "A heartthrob," my mother once described him, remembering. But weak also, a bit of a failure, teaching at the community college, not a real university, revelling in the crushes of adolescent girls there. A decent man but too willing to be a character, a clown. I feel the familiar pangs of impatience, even shameful hate, then a compensating rush of love and loss. His head is tilted back. He is in the middle of a large yawn, except his eyes are open, staring at the ceiling. His expression is one of horror. His ears are black.

"Anyone at all you can think of, Allen?" Wertz asks.

"He'd have to have access," Anderson adds. "The door was locked. And there would have to be motive. Nothing was taken."

"I don't know anything," I repeat, still staring. His eyes are locked on what? Something hovering above him. I remember the old superstition that a victim's eyes reflect his murderer, the last thing he sees. "Can I take these?"

"What!" It's the first time I've seen Anderson surprised. "No, you may not take them. They're police property. Why would you want them anyway?"

"Souvenirs," Wertz laughs.

"I don't have any pictures of him."

"Well, you don't want to remember him by these, now do you?"

"I guess not." I look around. "Then what am I here for ?"

"To bury your father."

"I mean—"

"We're looking for some assistance, Allen," Anderson sighs.

"Why?" I ask. "What difference does it make?"

"Between murder and suicide? All the difference in the world."

"He's still dead."

"I'd sleep easier at night if I knew why."

"Would you?"

"Things don't just happen," Anderson frowns. "Out of thin air, I mean."

"Of course they do."

"Now you don't believe that, either. You're just not yourself yet."

"When can I have the body?" I ask.

"We'll release it tomorrow, if you like. You have to arrange with a funeral home to pick it up."

"I'll do that."

He holds his hands out flat, like a dealer with no more cards. They both get up and lead me from the cubicle, Anderson and Wertz in front. As we leave, I grab one of the photos, jam it in my pocket.

The library has video machines, Walkmans, compact discs, even computer software. It's not until further back the stacks begin. I climb stairs past the encyclopedia up to where Literature is now hidden, breathe in the dust that sifts down from tan metal shelves. I have not felt the mute, healing quality of books in years. A small window at the end of the aisle looks over a large, featureless lawn. Staring at the million blades of grass, I sniff hard, crying unheard tears. They stream down my face, not beading on the skin but making a sheen. I wipe them away with my sleeve.

"Can I help you?" one of the teenage interns asks.

I hadn't noticed her standing on a little stepladder. Her brown skirt and white blouse blend into the books like a moth on dead leaves. I remember these girls, the ones who worked in the library after school and in summer. They were serious-looking, with glasses and stockings. This one is the same, her long brown hair parted simply in the middle and going halfway down her back.

"I'm sorry," I say. "I'm allergic to dust."

"Me too." She wrinkles her nose.

"Do you know where this belongs?" I show her the book.

"Is it overdue?" Her back is hunched like an old lady's, shoulders up around her ears. "Then you'll have to pay. It's only five cents a day."

"It's not mine," I explain, coming up to her. "I found it, cleaning up. I just want to put it back where it was. Is that all right?"

She smiles. Her face is characterless. Brown eyes behind brown-rimmed glasses. A small nose. A perfectly blank forehead to which nothing has happened yet.

I hand her the book.

"I think it goes up there. Ancient History."

She frowns, concentrating, then stretches to shelve it. Her body arches, reaching so high it forgets to guard its secrets. I can see the perfect inward curve below her ribs, the small ankles, the brown ripple of hair that comes down much longer than I thought, almost to her waist. Without thinking I hold each hip, as if grasping the handles of a chalice. I want to lift her high, to that last shelf where the oldest and dustiest books are. But she's surprisingly corporeal, heavier than I expect. She gives a little scream and comes telescoping down, suddenly human again, struggling. Her blouse comes out from the top of her skirt. For a moment my hand touches cold, goose-pimply flesh.

"Shhh!" someone calls from the first floor.

"I'm sorry," I whisper. "I was just trying to help."

She is rearranging herself, blushing, tucking in her blouse.

"That's OK," she mumbles, looking down at her shoes. I look with her. They are shiny and black.

"What's your name?"

"Pamela," she says. "Pam."

"Pam, how old are you? Sixteen?"

"Almost."

"My name is Allen Stanley. I used to live here."

"You mean you're not a member of the library?"

"No."

"Then how can you take out books?"

"It's not mine. I told you, I'm cleaning up after someone."

"Why can't they do it themselves?" she asks.

"It's my father's book. He died. I found it by his bed."

"Oh. I'm sorry." She looks at me. "What's your name again?"

"Allen Stanley."

"Is your dad the one who lives on Oakdale Drive?"

"That's right."

"Wow."

"You know about him?"

She nods. When her head stops, her hair picks up the movement and sways lower down, brushing the waist of her skirt.

"How did you hear about it?" I ask.

"Everybody knows," she says. "It's big news."

"What do they say?"

"Say about what?"

"My father."

"Nothing," she shrugs, suddenly reluctant. "Just that he . . . you know."

42

"Killed himself."

"Yes."

"But what else?"

"Nothing."

"Are you sure?"

"I don't get it," she frowns. "What do you mean, what else?"

"I want to know what people think." Without realizing what I've done I am touching her again, holding her shoulders, not shaking her but framing her in my gaze, trying to impart the sudden urgency I feel. "What do they think happened?"

"Excuse me, but . . . Allen?"

"Yes?"

"I'm not supposed to talk to my friends when I'm working here."

"Oh." I let go of her, looking around to see if there's a supervisor, some reason for her tone to go so strict and formal.

"But I can see you outside and talk to you there," she continues. "I get off at one. We close early in the summer."

"I know."

"So we can talk then."

"Where will we go?"

"Do you have a car?"

"Yes."

"Great!" She smiles and gives a little wave, even though we are less than a foot apart. "I'll put your book away for you now."

"Pam—"

"Shhh." She puts a finger to her lips, then climbs the ladder again.

At one, I stop in front of the library, wait while a few ladies from the circulation desk come out. A man in a uniform, the janitor, locks the twin front doors. He tests them once, rattles them, then goes on his way to the other offices of the Municipal Center.

"Hi!" She's standing next to the car, right by my window. "Didn't you see me?"

"No."

"That's because I changed."

It's true. She's in jeans and a T-shirt. Even her hair is different. It's bunched and passed through a small cloth ring before it spreads out again and flows around her shoulders, her bare arms.

"Come on in."

"OK."

She's playful now, running around the car and pushing off against the hood so her sneakered feet leave the ground. I put the seat back and stretch, driving.

"Where do you live, Pam?"

"Oh, let's not go there."

She won't sit. She perches on her knees, holds the headrest and hangs on.

"Where do you want to go?"

"Just drive."

I am again convinced the suburbs are a stage set, as houses on either side repeat themselves like the scenery band in a bad play. Every fourth or fifth gap reveals a turquoise block of swimming pool, or an alley of garish flowers, huge marigolds, Day-Glo tulips, one particularly popular hybrid that looks like a bulbous, pastel-colored cone of sores. Pam bounces on the seat, still kneeling, regarding all this as if it's new.

"I'll be able to drive soon," she says.

"You will?"

"Uh-huh. Maybe you could teach me."

"You know, you shouldn't be doing this with strange men."

"Doing what?"

"Getting into their cars, I mean."

"I know." She looks at me seriously, a flash of that unnatural, grownup side I saw in the library. "But you wanted to talk and it's better if people don't see us together."

"Why?"

"Slow down."

I'm only going forty, but it's one of those winding developments where the roads try to make the maximum use of their space by forming a spaghetti tangle of useless knots and intersections.

"Because of your dad," she says. "Because of what people say about him."

"What do they say?"

"That he was weird."

"Weird? How?"

"Well, he lived all alone, right?"

"Yes."

"In a house that was for a whole family?"

"That's true."

"And he was retired?"

quickly on the sidewalk, almost running. Her hair bounces at each step. I slow as I pass, but the girl I glimpse in the side mirror could be anyone. She is suddenly unrecognizable, generic. The car slides through an eternal present, passing the same house over and over.

"Ready?"

"Yes."

The light from the hallway cast her face in shadow. She was almost invisible. I could smell her though, as she sat on my bed. The mattress tilted and I flowed toward her.

"What's that?" I sniffed.

"It's soap. Sandalwood soap." She pushed her hair. It fell back, so silky, a glowing cascade that broke over her shoulder. "Do you want anything?"

"No."

"Good." She looked around, then back to the door.

"Where are you going?"

"Nowhere," she said. "I'll stay here as long as you want."

"It's not soap," I insisted, sniffing again.

"It's perfume," she admitted. "Are you going to have nightmares?"

"No."

She reached out and brushed my temple with her fingers. They burned, left glowing trails in my skin. I yawned and rolled over, staring straight up.

"You're pretty old to be afraid of the dark, you know."

"I can see molecules," I announced, opening my eyes wide.

"No you can't. They're too small."

"I can. Here they come now." Swimming particles, floating in a black sea.

"They're too small," her voice came again, as she got up. The earth moved, the mattress going level. "Molecules are what everything's made of. You can't see them."

"Why do you have to go?"

"I'm not going anywhere. I'll be right outside."

I turned as she opened the door. The light flared from the hall. She wore a black dress that stopped uncertainly above her knees. Her perfume hung so thick in the air my eyes teared.

"Go to sleep," she said. "Don't be afraid, OK?"

"OK."

"Don't dream," she warned.

Later, in the part of the night that has no name, I got up, my feet cold on the floor. The lights were off. I poked my nose into the fresh air of the hallway.

"Melissa?"

The door to her room was open, the blackness slightly more gray where it showed the empty bed. One dresser drawer gaped. I went slowly back out, hands in front to ward off objects. Walls, doors, the floor itself terrified me. I was beginning to grow, and never knew where my body was, where it began and ended, what it was doing there. I gripped the bannister and went downstairs, calling her name in a voice so low she could not possibly have heard, trying to conjure her up out of the dark, wishing her into existence.

"Melissa?"

What was the dream that terrified me awake? I had al-

49

ready forgotten. Or was this it now? Down more steps, my bare feet on the freezing tiles. Finally it occurred to me to turn on a light. I flicked the switch and blinked, blind, then took my hands away from my face and was staring at the door to the broom closet. The vacuum cleaner, where my mother superstitiously kept the household cash, stuck partway out, its end popped open, empty. I knelt by it, stuck my finger in the soft white rubber seal to the dustbag, comforted myself with that strangely sensual touch.

"Melissa?"

The house and I, sole survivors, confront each other. I still haven't bought food. The plastic portions frozen by my mother over the years are the only things to eat. The refrigerator is stuffed with condiments and all those strange clear tasteless sodas old people drink: seltzer, club, tonic, quinine. I unfold the smoking cold foil and find a hamburger, already cooked. "7/4," July Fourth, grill marks of a long-ago barbecue still seared into the frozen meat.

The phone rings.

"You settling in?"

It takes me a moment, though Sally's heartland twang is a dead giveaway.

"Still recovering from last night," I say. "How about you?"

"Last night's all hearsay to me. I don't remember a thing. Should I?"

"Not if you don't want to."

"Well I do, actually. Remember, that is." Her voice goes low and confidential. "B-o-b is still here."

"Bob?"

"He leaves in about an hour. What are you doing for dinner?"

"I was just heating something up."

"Oh." She's disappointed. "That's a shame. I was going to invite you over."

"I don't think I can take two nights in a row with you, Sally."

"That's just what B-o-b said after our first date."

"Why do you spell out his name like that?"

" 'Cause it's in code that way," she yawns. "You're kind of slow tonight, aren't you, Allen?"

"I am," I admit. "Early bedtime for me."

"Yeah, well, you just watch who you go driving with," she drawls. "We got laws here, you know. Involving the corruption of minors. Allen? Allen, you still there?"

"Of course I'm here."

"You sure you don't want to come over?"

"Not tonight, Sally."

I walk through the empty house and come again to the bedroom. It is the endpoint of any exploration. My parents' bed is so big. I try flopping down on it but the mattress doesn't give. Nestling deeper, determined, I can see through the open door into the bathroom. Not the tub, where the bloodstains remain like tea leaves at the bottom of a cup, but higher. I take out the photo I stole from Anderson and Wertz's office, try lining it up with reality, following my father's terror-wide stare. Then I see it. A smudge on the ceiling. I go into the bedroom and crouch, getting low, as close to the tub as I can without actually stepping into it, and look up. In the far corner, almost hidden, is daubed:

MES

Melissa Elizabeth Stanley.
  In blood.

chapter 3

SALLY IS OUT FRONT. IT'S SO hot she wears a shirt ripped at the bottom and tied in a knot. Underneath I can see either a bikini top or a colored bra. That, along with a big sun hat and shorts, completes her gardening outfit. She holds a pair of shears and a bucket.

"You're a sight," she says. "You've got to upkeep yourself. Where did you sleep?"

"Downstairs. On the couch."

She spreads a towel over the ground and kneels, chopping at the low bushes on her side of our mutual border. She's trying to create some space between the grass and the foliage. They stand out like poodles' tails.

"I have to find an undertaker today. Do you know one?"

"Undertaker?" She shakes her head at my gaffe. "Fu-

53

neral director is what you want. And no, I don't. What do I look like, a crone?"

"I think there's only one. Down by the highway. Next to the supermarket."

"Is that what he is? Now I've been looking at that house for a year, trying to figure out what it's there for. Just says C. P. PLAYMORE out front, doesn't it? Like a private dwelling."

"He lives there too."

"Oh." She goes back to clipping. "Well, since you know the answer to a question before you ask it, why are you still standing there?"

"I'm wondering if you could come along."

"Me?"

"It would make it easier."

"I don't know," she says, getting up and patting the wrinkles out of her knees. "I'd have to change."

"Why?"

"Why? Because I can't go to a funeral parlor looking like something out of Beach Blanket Bingo, that's why. You just stay right there."

Waiting for her, I bend down and finger some of the branches she's cut. Their stiff, shiny green prickles seem utterly unlike anything in nature, as if they've been bred to mimic plastic.

"See you met Gorgeous George," she grins, dressed black as an Italian widow now, as we drive down to the highway.

"You spend all day watching the street, Sally?"

"It's better than TV, most times."

"What is it about this place?" I complain. "The whole atmosphere here seems drenched in sexuality."

"Huh?"

"And why does he have a key to the garage?" I go on quickly. "That's just like having a key to the front door."

"George loved your dad. Your dad treated him like—"

"A son?"

"No. But he liked him a whole lot. They'd talk."

"How do you know all this?"

"Because I'm alive in this, the twentieth century, and I have a brain."

"You're a snoop."

"So just who specifically do you mean when you say drenched in sexuality?"

"No one. That's the point. We're all just drowning in this liquor."

"My!"

"This essence of hunger and desire," I go on, unable to stop. "Don't you feel it?"

"People are bored. It's hot. Kids are out of school," she says matter-of-factly.

"What about me?"

"You're a wild card." She pats my leg. "You don't belong here. A single man living in a big house. Maybe that's why you see it more. Whatever it is that you see. To me it's just life in the 'burbs."

"And you like it?"

"It's what I signed on for."

"How is B-o-b?"

"Who? Oh, he's fine. Sleeping like a baby."

spLit – LEVELs

• • •

C. P. Playmore's is an aluminum-sided mansion over-looking the shopping center. Playmore's was here first, a big white house, immaculately kept up, with a border of topiary shielding the windows and the front porch. There's a sloping gravel driveway leading to a big lawn that serves as a parking lot.

"You ever come here before?" she asks, as we gun up the hill, spraying gravel.

"Once, for my mother."

"You're a good son," she says, oddly, offering me strength I didn't know I needed.

We get out and ring the brass-plated bell. It chimes in-side.

"May I help you?"

"Corky?" I ask.

He's my age, with a starved look, an all-skull head and huge hands taped to insubstantial, bony wrists.

"I am Timothy Playmore," he admits.

"Allen Stanley, remember?"

"Allen?" He peers at me as if through thick gloom, then seems to recall. "Of course. How are you, Allen? And this must be Mrs. Stanley."

"It must," Sally says dryly.

"Come in, come in."

He turns all the way around and walks briskly away, like a salesman does when he knows you're going to fol-low, not social at all. Our feet are swallowed in carpet. The house is made to give the appearance of a "private dwelling," as Sally would say, but there are weird industrial touches—plastic signs reminding you not to smoke, fire doors in between open rooms—that make you realize it's under a different set of regulations.

"Corky," I call, trying to get him to slow down, "I thought you were going to be a doctor."

"Well I am, in a way," he throws over his shoulder, taking us to the far corner of the mansion. "I do the work, you see."

"You mean the . . . ?"

"Embalming." He finally turns, grinning to reveal what look like baby teeth. His hair is thin and fair, almost golden.

It's a small office done in bright red, with a thick bristly carpet, gold tassels hanging off the lampshade, and pukey green landscapes in elaborate frames. Corky sits behind a massive desk and motions for us to settle on a facing sofa. Sally spreads her legs and knots her hands in a clump between them.

"Mr. and Mrs. Stanley," he begins.

"Corky, this isn't—"

"We're looking for something cheap," Sally says, reaching onto the desk and taking a large looseleaf notebook.

"I remember your husband from long ago," he smiles, talking to Sally but staring at me. "He was a very morose, unpleasant boy."

"Was he?"

She's flipping through the plastic-coated photos of caskets.

"I'm so sorry about your father, Allen."

"Thank you."

"Don't thank me until I've repaired the damage. When you see him next, he'll look like the groom on a wedding cake."

"Do you have a price list?" Sally asks.

He passes her a simple photocopied sheet.

"They keep going up," he apologizes. "No point in getting it printed. I can see the little woman takes care of things for you."

"Is your father—?"

"Dead," he nods. "I did him myself. Not easy, either. All those years of drinking. I had to inject talcum powder under the nose."

"I'm sorry."

"I found it quite liberating, actually." He spreads his arms to indicate the surroundings, as if he'd inherited a lavish pleasure palace, not a funeral home. "Maybe you will too."

"Here." She points to the simplest one. "Can you afford this?"

"I guess," I say slowly. "What does he need Bronze Sure-Grip handles for?"

"Very useful at the interment. You don't want to cause a scene. With those cheap handles I've seen the coffin dropped in at a tilt. At one funeral the poor woman's casket was wedged into the plot at a forty-five-degree angle. They had to jump on it to get her to lie flat."

"When can it be ready?"

"Friday."

"That's the day after tomorrow."

He looks at me.

"You have a reason to stay longer?"

58

"No."

"It's customary to lay the deceased to rest as soon as possible. Better for the survivors as well."

We go over a few more things, sign the papers. When he leads us out, again walking briskly ahead of us, I notice he's almost bowlegged, as if he spent years riding a horse. He steps in wide half-circles around a central void.

"It was good to see you, Corky." I shake his dead-fish hand.

"They just call me Mr. Playmore now."

He stands at the door, frowning as we cut across his lawn.

"What a creep!" Sally laughs. "You OK, Allen?"

"I'm fine."

"Hey, that was fun being your wife. Where do you know that guy from, anyway?"

"School. Corky Playmore was the first boy in school to wear long hair."

"Was he?"

"For a while. He's grown up . . . differently than I would have thought."

"Him and everybody else, huh? Where to now?"

"Wherever you want."

"That would be the liquor store."

The old shopping center has grown decrepit since it was upstaged by an indoor mall a few exits down the highway. There is just a row of shops connected by a cracked sidewalk, grass sprouting through the concrete in summer profusion. A huge parking lot yawns in front, more abandoned shopping carts than cars. The supermarket is the one big building, then the liquor store, a pizzeria, and a beauty parlor. She leads me to the Cork and Bottle. At first I think it's the beauty parlor we've wandered into by mistake. There are high black stools bolted into the worn carpeting all along the counter.

"What's the matter?" Sally asks, then turns. "Hello, Johnny."

A fat man behind the register nods at me, maybe imperceptibly raises his eyebrows, and smiles.

"I don't remember this," I say.

"They put the stools in later, I'll bet." She sits on the one closest to the register and twirls, explaining: "Allen was born here."

"You were, huh? Me too." The fat man is on a wooden chair behind the register. His soft, pink-white skin makes it hard to guess his age. A huge belly sticks out and rests on the keys. His shirt has grease marks from their metal stems. Everything is old-fashioned here. "You probably recognize some of these bottles, then. Hell, they were here when I bought the place."

"I was never in here."

"Oh sure you were. With a fake ID probably. All the kids do it. I put the stools in myself. That's what confuses you. Change in the state law. We're allowed to have five stools in a package store."

This time he winks, even puts his finger to the side of his nose, a sly vaudeville gesture, then nods down to Sally.

"What'll the lady have?"

"A Cape Cod," Sally says. "That's a nice morning drink."

"What's that?"

60

"Johnny knows. Cranberry juice and vodka. Sit down."
She sets the next stool twirling. "We just been to see
C. P. Playmore, Johnny. He ever come in here?"

"That fairy? I think he's too busy drinking formalde-
hyde."

"What'll you have, Allen?"

"Nothing."

She pouts.

"Then why'd we come?"

I am looking at the bottles. They line the wall up to
the ceiling. Some are incredibly dusty. Behind the
counter a little makeshift bar is assembled, the cheapest
of house brands in plastic bottles with built-in pourers,
refilled from a central vat, no doubt. With a professional
air the fat man makes Sally her crimson drink.

"You don't have to pay," I say, staring as she hands him
a ten-dollar bill.

"Oh I must." She tosses her head back and takes a long
swallow. I watch her shiny throat pulsate in the heat.
When she puts the glass back down, it's empty. "If I
drink alone, I pay," she says, then nods to the fat man.

"Another?"

"Make sure it's diet cranberry juice," she murmurs, her
voice already soothed. "I'm watching my figure."

"Now what"—he puffs, bending over a small refrigerator—"could a pretty woman like you possibly be wanting
diet cranberry juice for?"

"Cystitis," she giggles.

"What?"

"Never mind. Allen, shit or get off the pot."

"Vodka, no ice," I decide, moving to sit next to her,

mounting the bar stool from behind. I put a twenty-dollar bill on the counter.

"No, no," Sally says, pushing it back. "My party."

"Lot of people come by here?" I ask the fat man.

He has, without asking, poured himself one and dragged his chair closer to us. I am fascinated by the way his buttons are splayed. He is wearing a white undershirt. It sticks out in bumps through the gaps.

"Mostly housewives," he says.

"Wife to a house," Sally embroiders dreamily.

"And working men. Sometimes they just stop in for a quickie. Without the bar, I'd be out of business. Discount houses take all the shoppers."

"Did my father ever come in here? David Stanley?"

He nods noncommittally, takes his drink. His nails are tiny chips of calcium buried in pink fat.

"What was that name again?"

"Stanley. Up on Oakdale Drive. Did my father ever come in?"

"Oh, Allen," Sally sighs, looking deep into her drink. "You've committed another social blunder."

"Have I?"

Johnny takes a dainty sip and puts his glass down.

"He came in. Part of his walk. At least I think so. What's a constitutional? That's what he always called it."

"A constitutional is a daily walk," Sally states. "First prize: one drink."

She holds her hands up over her head like a prize-fighter. From where Johnny sits he can make it without moving off his stool. While he leans down to get the cranberry juice, Sally suddenly comes alive, grips my

arm, and shakes her head violently, mouthing, "No, no."
Then, as soon as he hauls himself up, she's back slumped
over the counter, licking her lips.

"Your dad took a walk every Saturday morning," the
fat man resumes. "Used to buy some items at the store
and then stop in here."

"Did he say anything?"

"We'd chat."

"About what?"

"God, I hate you!" Sally says. "You didn't need me
back there at all, did you?"

"I was just asking—"

"Just using me is all. Just wanted me to lead you someplace." She stands, sways a moment, holding the glass
like she's about to throw it. "I get all dolled up, baby-sit
you through the funeral arrangements, then buy you a
drink. But all you're really interested in is talking to
Fatso here about your kinky father."

"My what?"

"Never mind." She puts the glass back down on the
counter, gently. "I'm sorry, Johnny."

"Been called worse," the fat man replies, unperturbed.

He rings up the drinks on the old machine and pushes
the change back. It's not enough to pick up.

"What do you mean, kinky?" I ask.

"I'll be waiting in the car," she mutters. The door
tinkles as it shuts.

"Born here, huh?" the fat man muses. "Not many
people can say that."

I stare at the money on the plastic-topped bar, the
rings of water, the glasses suddenly dirty in daylight.

"My folks sold their place, moved to Florida," he goes on. "So when I came back, I didn't have no home to go to."

"Why do it, then?" I ask. The bottles on the wall are familiar yet unreadable, like rows of hieroglyphs. Except one I recognize, the slave boy decanter from last night.

"Huh?" He looks up, eyes deeply set in his amiable face.

"Why come home? You said you left, didn't you?"

"Oh, I was gone for years."

"What did you do?"

"This and that. Made my pile."

"Then what?"

"Then I came back and sank it all into this dump," he laughs.

"Why?"

"Guess I couldn't stay away." He belches philosophically, pouring himself another drink. "You know, some people here didn't like your dad. But I figure where a man puts his dingus is his own affair."

"His what?"

"I think your friend out there is weeping."

She is waiting on Playmore's mound of green, plopped down under a carved bush.

"Come on, Sally."

I hold out my hand. She doesn't take it.

"I am watching an American landscape," she says, nodding at the highway.

"You're drunk."

"Yes, but in the morning I will be smart again."

"It still is morning."

"See?"

She pushes herself up but stumbles. I catch her and hold her in my arms.

"Slick," she murmurs, melting against me. "You put this mountain here just for me to fall?"

"Isn't Bob worried about you?"

"He certainly is. I suppose that's my subinterior motivation."

I get her in the passenger side, crunch around the gravel, then back slowly down the hill.

"Tell me about my father. What do you mean, kinky?"

"Oh nothing."

We're about to get on the road. I stop the car, turn off the engine.

"It's hot," she complains. "God, I feel sick."

"You drank too much, too fast."

"Thank you, Doctor Albert Schweitzer."

"We're not moving until you tell me about my father."

"I can't tell you about him unless we're moving," she sighs. "It's easier to talk in a moving car, don't you think? The words just trail away, like smoke out a window, instead of choking everybody up."

So we drive. I give her five full minutes. Then, just as I'm about to get angry, she begins.

"Everybody knows the reason your dad killed himself."

"Why?"

"Because he was out of control."

"What was he doing?"

"Lusting after little girls." She turns to me with a clumsy, drunken leer. "I mean, not toddlers, but . . . young girls."

"He was sixty-seven."

"Yeah. Disgusting, isn't it?"

"It's not true."

"What do you think he was doing at the Cork and Bottle every Saturday?"

"You mean people go there to . . . ?"

"Sure. Johnny's got this room in back. It's not much, just a bed. But he rents it out for extra money. Rents it out by the hour."

"How do you know this?"

" 'Cause I've been there some myself."

Unconsciously, she has assumed the position of what she implies. Her body is laid almost flat, her legs spread, her eyes have that glazed, vacant expression, not staring past me but staring nowhere, focused on infinity.

"Why do you have to go there if Bob's away all day teaching school?"

"I wouldn't let these types into my home," she says indignantly. "Besides, there's something titillating about doing it in the shopping center, don't you think? And near all that liquor too."

"Did you go back there with my father?"

"Jesus, no! You have a vivid imagination. These were just some affairs of the heart. And I said he was after *young* girls, much as I value the compliment."

"Did you ever see him with anyone?"

"No."

"Then how—?"

"It ain't the place you go with some blue-haired lady from the Old Folks Center, if you get my drift. He was having himself a time, the old goat."

"But with little girls?"

"He did have that reputation, didn't he?"

I stop the car in the middle of the road. We are in front of our two houses. I can see, she is tilted so far back, one ring notched in her neck. I have one myself, a mark of incipient middle age. The way a lumberjack notches a tree, marks it for harvesting, then goes on his way knowing when he comes back all the leaves will have withered and the branches died.

"How did you hear that?"

"People talk," she shrugs. "Especially when they heard what he did to himself."

"It's not true," I repeat. "But even if it was, that's no reason."

"Just seems like an act of desperation, doesn't it? I mean, we mature women have so much more to offer."

"He wasn't having sex with anyone."

"How do you know?"

"I knew him."

"Did you?"

"I'm his son."

"I guess I just heard things. Stupid gossip, probably." She touches my shoulder, gives it a friendly squeeze. "I didn't mean to upset you."

"It was good to have you with me at the funeral parlor," I say. "I didn't take you along just for the ride."

"Well, I wouldn't mind being taken for a ride by you," she smiles.

Then she's out of the car, walking calmly to her house. She doesn't seem drunk anymore. Along the driveway and sidewalk there is a fringe of cut grass, slowly dying.

George has come back and manicured my trees, my bushes. It all looks perfect.

"Don't be afraid," a voice calls, as I come in.

Upstairs, Anderson and a thin, European-looking man with an elegant face and a pencil mustache are crowded into the bathroom, craning their necks at the ceiling.

"Got your message," Anderson says, not looking down. "This here's Forensic."

At least that's how I hear his name, it goes so well with his face. He gets up on the toilet seat and examines the scrawl more closely.

"Lefty," he says.

"You think so?"

His hands almost brush the dried blood, like an art restorer or a connoisseur.

"Done with the finger. We may be able to get some prints off this, at the end of each stroke."

"How could you have missed it?" I ask.

Anderson shrugs.

"Like I said, this kind of investigation is not our specialty."

"All you had to do was look up."

"You've been a great help, Allen."

"This means he did it himself," I say.

"Does it? Because of your sister?" He glares at me. "Yeah, I know about her. I asked you for help before. How come you didn't tell me what happened here?"

"It's private. Besides, it was twenty years ago."

"Could have been yesterday"—he nods at the ceiling—"far as he was concerned."

"I didn't want it all brought up again. What's the point now?"

"The point? Come here, I'll show you the point." He leads me back into the hallway, his muscular frame filling the space, just as Forensic is taking out a large flash camera. "Know where this is?"

We are standing in front of another door.

"Melissa's room," I say.

"You been in?"

"No."

"Not once?"

"Not for years."

"Even now, when you came back?"

I shake my head.

He opens his fist. There's a piece of cloth inside.

"You recognize this?" It's woman's underwear, panties, lacy and shiny. "There's clothes in there."

"Well of course there are. I told you, no one's been in that room for years."

"They're new. Name brands, models, price tags still on some. We checked. All for a young girl. What do you know about that?"

"Nothing."

He sighs.

"I am trying to do right by you. But you are not being cooperative. Now who used this room?"

"No one. No one went inside it after she died."

"Did you hear what you said? You said after your sister died."

"Of course. Melissa is dead."

"Do you know that?"

69

"No. Not for a fact. But I have to believe it," I say. "My father couldn't. That's why he did what he did."

"Twenty years later? That doesn't make sense."

"What does?"

"Maybe he died because it was all starting up again. That's what it looks like to me."

"What's starting up again? What do you mean?"

"I mean this, dammit." He doesn't know what to do with the panties, stuffs them awkwardly in his coat pocket.

"Nothing happened here. Nothing ever happens here," I repeat. "It's the middle of nowhere."

"Tomorrow I'll get the files out. Your sister fits into this all right, but I'll be damned if I can see how."

"Hey, Harley!" a voice comes from downstairs.

He turns, distracted.

"Yeah?"

Wertz comes up and grins at me.

"The lady says she went with him to the funeral home. You know, Playmore's. Then they drove around for an hour. Just talked."

"About what?" He asks Wertz, not me.

"Said he needed a shoulder to cry on. She was being a good neighbor."

Anderson nods.

"I had to wake up her husband," Wertz adds casually. "He seemed kind of pissed off."

We are all standing in the hallway when the flash camera starts clicking rapidly away. It gives a stroboscopic quality to our frozen poses.

After they leave, I walk around the house picking at my

dirty clothes. I want to bathe, feel my body go weightless and warm in the soapy tub. Forcing myself, I get a bucket, a big sponge, and strip in front of the mirror. I find in my eyes an expression of stunned neutrality.

The phone rings. Rather than skirt the huge bed I lie across it, naked, and reach the night table by my father's side.

"Hello?"

There's no answer.

"Is anyone there?"

"Is that you?" she asks.

"Sally?"

A pause.

"No. It's Pam, from the library. Remember me?"

"How did you get my number?"

"From the phone book, silly. I called before, but other people kept answering."

"What did you say to them?"

"Nothing. I hung up."

God knows what they made of that.

"Listen," she says. "I have news."

"Pamela, it was wrong of me to ask you those questions the other day. You shouldn't go around—"

"But I found stuff out."

"What?"

"Wait a minute," she whispers. There is a muffled exchange in the background, the sound of the phone's plastic clunking. "OK," she announces, back on.

"Who was that?"

"My mom."

"Where are you calling from?"

spLit-LEVELs

"The kitchen. Listen, I'm going to the movies tonight with some friends."

"Good."

"But not really." Her voice goes stagy with intrigue and melodrama.

"No, Pamela."

"Pick me up at the parking lot in front of the high school. At six."

"What did you find out?"

"I can't tell you now. Just trust me, OK?"

My pale body lies under the blank white ceiling.

"I got to go," she says. "Are you coming or not?"

She hangs up before I can answer.

The impetus to clean, to start afresh, is gone. I can only plunge into a sound, dreamless nap, being careful to set the alarm first.

I began asking myself, who are these people? This woman weeping at the kitchen table, her hands smooth with worry. This man clutching the wheel, wide-eyed, as if staring into a wind tunnel. Only Melissa I knew, loved. And she was gone. My mother had waited all evening, calling, pacing. Now it was night. My father came home only to turn and go again. Why did he take me? Sitting on the front seat, somehow immune to panic, I watched him as he scanned the sides of the road, as he came close to hitting the car ahead of us.

"Don't look at me," he said, and reached over, turned my head like it was on a swivel.

I watched the road go by, the berserk vegetation.

It's like always, I wanted to tell him. She goes out but

72

she comes back. Don't you know? Why are you so worried this time? Nights now, when you sleep, she goes away. I smell her in the morning, her late return, her perfume still in the air mixing with breakfast. Sandalwood and bacon. Don't you know? He was searching from side to side again, not watching out for what was right in front of him. I saw his face as something that existed apart from me, a man suddenly aged.

Later, he would take me on longer rides, terrible searches into the city. We would say nothing, going in. It was summer and he kept his window all the way down, air blasting through the car, pushing his hair back against his skull. I kept my window shut, staring out, my nose bouncing off the cool glass.

We drove in ever-widening circles around the bus station. Green, yellow, red, all against a background of neon blackness. He went trolling down those side streets, his arm hanging out the window, palm loose against the metal body of the car. When they would come over, the girls, two at a time, they would stoop low, their hair and faces—elaborately teased and painted like tropical birds—level with the low-cut tops of their blouses, their exposed breasts. I stared from deep in the shadows, never invisible enough, all the way at the other end of the seat.

"Why are you looking for her?" they'd ask, when he'd show them the picture. He never let them touch it. He'd hold it out in front of him, stiff, like a priest with his cross fending off vampires.

"She's my daughter."

"Yeah?" They'd look at him, suspicious. "Who's he?"

spLit-LEVELS

"My son."

One laughed. I saw it from her point of view, how these words—son, daughter—the relationships they implied, had no meaning here. Others were more friendly. "Pretty," they'd say. Or wave at me. "Hello," one smiled, perfectly ordinary, sincere. My heart melted. He'd give them money, twenty dollars each, and wait for them to bring their friends. A whole world existed just beyond the lights. I watched as they walked away, their thighs, their sheer stockings, winking in and out of the dark. They vanished completely for a moment, in a doorway or around a corner, then returned with another, high heels strangely silent, so deeply was I burrowing into the glass, steel, and vinyl of the car.

Going home after these futile nights, he still kept his window open. I would fall asleep and breathe in the taste of pure exhaust. Like meat.

Even though it's summer, the school parking lot is still the place to be. Across the flat expanse groups of cars are parked, others move slowly, all with music blaring out their windows. Heat ripples give the scene a hellish, baked quality, this paved and patched landscape with its fading white lines. At 6:15 I turn off the engine.

"Hey, Mr. S. What are you doing here?"

Mr. S?

In a sporty white car with red seats, something hanging over the dashboard, Gorgeous George casually screeches to a halt beside my window. His radio is going as loud as the lawn mower was the other morning. The kid must thrive on noise.

"Did I do a good job?" he calls.

He is at ease in his car, a centaur leaning back on its own horse-torso, toying with the engine, which roars its approval. He has mirrored glasses and a fluorescent baseball cap. I only recognize him because of his shaggy hair and torn sleeves.

"Job?" I ask.

"The extra yard work. Didn't you notice?"

"Oh. It was great, George. What are you doing here?"

He lifts his arm and reveals a girl, so cuddled up against his side I didn't see her before. She looks at me with sulky, suspicious eyes.

"George," I ask, thinking of the clothes in Melissa's room. "Did you ever see anyone at the house? Besides my father?"

He frowns.

"You mean like a ghost?"

"No, not a ghost. A person. A houseguest, I mean. Someone staying overnight."

"No people in that house," he says. "Just your dad. Once I saw the gas man reading the meter. Does that count?"

"Thanks, George. I was just wondering."

"Should I come again?" he asks. "Next week?"

"Sure."

"OK. Later."

The car shoots off, slides smoothly between a parked conversation with about an inch to spare on each side, and stops again, for more socializing.

"You know him?"

Pamela is once again standing by my window. I am

75

staring into her belly button. She's wearing a skimpy top and an elastic pair of shorts.

"He mows my lawn. Is he a friend of yours?"

"No. He's a senior. Move over."

I do, without thinking. She sits in front of the wheel and pretends to steer, beeps the horn by accident and jumps back.

"How are you, Pamela?"

"I'm OK. You look terrible."

She puts the back of her hand to my cheek. All her gestures seem so learned. This is her mother, seeing if someone has a temperature.

"You look pretty."

"Thanks. It's hot!" She takes all her hair and twists it up into a flip, then lets it fall. She has shaved her armpits. "So, can I drive?"

"Do you have a license?"

"No. But I'll get a Learner's Permit in a few days."

"Then that's when you can drive."

"Oh, come on."

"Look," I say, pointing to the cop car which ceaselessly patrols the parking lot. Every once in a while he will pull in to roust people. All the cars will start up and scatter like a flock of birds disturbed, to resettle here a half hour later.

"Then let's go someplace empty," she says. "And I can drive there."

"Maybe."

We switch positions. She pushes herself over me like I'm a log.

"Someplace empty?" I ask.

"I know where."

We drive away from the highway, past the last developments to where the original countryside still exists. It's
on its way out, though. Farmhouses, stripped of their
land, rot next to parcelled-off plots. They lay the roads
out first, before the split-levels, so it seems a safe place
for her to drive, smooth new blacktop and no cars. I
move over, but keep my feet on the pedals and my hands
just above hers.

"Don't be so nervous," she chides. "You're shaking.
Faster!"

"Do you know where we're going?"

"Of course."

She turns so abruptly we're both slung to the window.
I grab the wheel and straighten us out on the bumpy side
road.

"I have everything under control," she says. "Let me
drive."

It's the kind of coarse paving that comes away in
chunks. Clouds of dust follow us, obscuring the rearview
mirror. After a shack there is nothing for five hundred
yards, just stunted trees and bad soil, boulders thrown up
along the sides of the road by years of plowing.

"Here."

Her foot jams down on mine. It's the accelerator,
though, not the brake. We spurt forward and smack into
a tree.

The horn is blaring. I pull her off the wheel, gripping
her below the rib cage. The noise stops.

"Wow," she murmurs.

"Are you all right?"

"Uh-huh." She shakes her head. "Look at that."

We have knocked over a sapling. I get out to investigate. A thin, splintered trunk. I coax the car back onto the shoulder. The body just has some dents in it. Pam stands on the road, bends over to examine herself in the side mirror.

"Are you sure you're all right?"

"I'm fine. Did you ever come here before?" she asks.

"Here? No."

"Why? Didn't they know about the culvert then?"

"The what?"

"The culvert."

It's not clear if she even knows what the word means. She uses it like a place name.

"Come on. I'll show you."

She skips off, into the secondary-growth forest.

This was all farmland, I think again, having a tough time, getting whapped by branches she seems to slip right through. Then they let it grow over . . . not that long ago judging by the height of the trees, twenty or thirty years, when people like my family came. Where did they go, the farmers? We are heading downhill. The slope, suddenly steep, has me in a run. I grab at small trees as I go rushing down, unable to stop. Finally, at the edge of a stream, there is a big concrete post sunk deep into the ground.

"See?" she says, standing by the water. "It's the culvert." Then she adds, confidentially: "I had to ask directions on how to get here. It's my first time too."

But I am still trying to understand the incongruity of

poured concrete in the middle of these woods. It is new, white and sun-warmed, vaguely gritty. A powder from it comes off in my hand. The stream disappears into a large tunnel, a pipe at least five feet high, that runs under a road just above us. I peer up to see the back of an unfinished house, stickers still on the windows and glass doors.

"It's the back of a development," she says. "But I think they ran out of money or something, because it's been here for years. This is the drainage ditch."

There's a patch of long, unkempt grass where the sun breaks through, right at the stream's edge, even a few violets growing. She sits and pats the ground beside her.

"Who comes here?" I ask.

"People. For parties."

"Where are they now?"

"They'll probably come later," she says. "It's still light. Will you sit by me, please?"

I sit. She keeps touching her forehead.

"Are you hurt?"

"I hit my head against the windshield there."

"Let me see."

I brush her hair away. This is what I first noticed about her, the high, perfectly smooth forehead. Her long hair falls back over my fingers. I have to hold it out of the way.

"There *is* a spot. It might swell."

"I'm OK," she says.

A bird flies overhead. A crow. I can see it reflected in the brown pools of her eyes. They regard me directly, barely blinking, as the crow caws over and over.

"What did you find out about my father?"

She takes a deep breath.

"It's not about your father. It's about you."

"Me?"

"I have an uncle who's a policeman. He says he knows you."

"What's his name?"

"Uncle Steve."

"What's his last name?"

"I don't know," she shrugs.

"Wertz?"

"Oh, of course. How did you know that?"

"Never mind. What did he say?"

"He was talking to my mother yesterday. He's my mother's brother. He says someone called them about you."

"Called them? Where?"

"At the station. Some woman. She wouldn't say who she was. But she told them she saw you here a week ago."

"Saw me?"

"Here. In town."

The water from the stream rushes on, over rocks and discarded hunks of concrete.

"It's not true," I say. "I came here yesterday. No. The day before yesterday. But—"

"She says she saw you here a week ago. Just about the time they figure it happened."

"What happened?"

"You know. When your dad died. Uncle Steve says that's important."

"Why would that be important?"

She shrugs. Very elaborately. At first I think it's another learned gesture, a cartoonish hunching of the shoulders to indicate ignorance. But in fact she's pulling her arm through the sleeve of her tiny top. I stop her, arrest the motion of the bare flesh. But the material, freed, is under such tension that it shrinks to nothing. Her other arm reaches up and discards the fabric, lays it neatly beside her.

"Hold me?" she asks.

She glues herself to me, every particle of her flesh in contact with mine, arm to arm, leg to leg, like we are cookie-cutter dolls. One hand reaches down to unbuckle my belt.

"Pam—"

"I've never been with anyone before."

"Neither have I," I hear myself say. "Not like this."

"How does it work?" she asks, grabbing my penis.

"Jesus!"

"Sorry." She explores with more care. "Isn't it uncomfortable?"

"It's not always like that."

"Oh."

"This isn't right," I say.

"Why?"

I lie back to look at her, to find her eyes.

"Why?" she asks again, so serious, a schoolgirl waiting for explanation, waiting for logic.

When we kiss I'm tasting something new, beyond taste, more like a cold breeze blowing through me, sending shivers.

"It's very wrong," is all I can answer, mumbling against the softness of her lips.

"Are you going soon?" she asks, tightening her grip on me.

"Going away from here, you mean? I don't know."

"You should. You should go away as soon as you can."

"Why?"

"So you can take me with you."

"Why would you want to leave?"

"I hate it here."

"In a few years you can leave on your own."

"I want to go now. How did you get out?"

"After high school I went to college. I got a scholarship."

"But didn't you have to come back?"

"No. I worked vacations to make extra money. I never came back. Not until now."

She sits up, looks at me. "We better do it fast, before people come."

"I'm going to take you home."

"Why? Don't you want to stay?"

"No."

She looks away. I brush a tear out of her eye. Then she leaps on me like a playful dog and we roll, wrestling, down until we're in and out of the water. It's actually mild sewage we're soaking in. I can smell the algae bloom feeding off the detergents, the heavy chlorine they treat the water with to make it drinkable. Still, it is cool, and sweeps all doubts away for as long as I listen to it, concentrate on its sound and nothing else.

"Are you ready to go now?" I ask.

"OK."

She pops up, not seeming too disappointed, maybe

even relieved, and goes to the shore, puts on her shirt. Slow, feeling bruised and creaky by comparison, I follow her.

"I don't want you to feel sad," I call ahead, admiring how her weightless body propels itself up the hillside like an antelope.

"I understand," she says, waiting for me at the top. "I know with older men it takes them longer sometimes."

A few other cars, some I recognize from the high school parking lot, are ranged along the shoulder near ours.

"Why didn't we see them at the culvert?" I wonder.

"Sometimes they get high in the woods first."

While we ride, she snuggles down in my lap, staring up at me.

"So why should Uncle Steve care when you got here?"

"I don't know. It's probably nothing. I'm glad you told me, though."

"What should I call you?" she wonders.

Pine needles still stick to my skin. Her hair is wet in places.

"Call me Allen."

"I don't like Allen. Maybe I'll call you Honey. That's what my mom calls my stepdad."

"Where's your real dad?"

"In Alaska someplace. I don't remember him at all. Sometimes when my mom is really drunk she says she still loves him."

"Doesn't your stepdad mind?"

"No. He's cool."

"Don't call me Honey."

"Why not?"

"We're almost there. Where should I drop you?"

"It doesn't matter," she yawns. "Are you going home now?"

"No. I think I'll drive around a while."

"Can't I come with you?"

"I need to think, Pam."

"You can't really call me on the phone, can you?"

"I don't see how. I'm not sure we should do this again."

"Why? Aren't you happy?"

"Happy? I don't know."

"I'll call you. Or you can come by the library."

We're at the circle of asphalt where I left her before. She's not interested in kissing or even touching now. She gets out of the car and comes around to the driver's side.

"You know George, that senior?" she asks.

"Yes."

"Kind of weird that we saw him at the parking lot tonight."

"Why?"

"Well, that was his car next to ours at the culvert, too."

The moon shines beyond her shoulder. It glints off her hair.

"Goodnight, Pamela."

"Be careful," she says. "Honey."

chapter 4

"Yoo-hoo!"

Sometime during the night I must have rolled off the couch onto the floor. I wake staring at the heating vent, a small quarter-cylinder of windowed pipe running the length of the living room.

"Allen?"

I stretch out long and thin, my hands past my head, my feet straightened like a fish tail, trying to be a perfect shape, featureless and sexless, so the hot air will blow over me and stop my shivering. Then I remember it's summer. There's a leafy rustling. A face appears off to the side of the picture window.

"You up yet?"

"How did you know I was here?" I ask, lying so low I can see under Sally's chin, where a strange dimple or scar makes her face look buttoned-on.

"Spying," she admits frankly. "I knocked but you were out like a light."

"What time is it?"

"Past noon. Let me in, will you?"

I go to the door. Looking down, I see I'm barefoot. My feet have a brown stain on them, as if they've been dipped in coffee. Last night, Pam, the drainage ditch, the long aimless drive I took afterward, are all pushed just beyond the rim of my attention. I don't want to think.

"Jesus," she says, as soon as I open up. "I can see I'm going to have to assume command here. Take off your clothes."

"Not you too."

"What's that supposed to mean?"

"Nothing. What are you doing here, Sally?"

"I'm here to apologize."

"For what?"

"For yesterday, of course. But I'm not apologizing to no bum. Where's the shower?"

"There's one upstairs, by the other bedrooms."

"Good. I'll keep you company."

They peel off like skin, my clothes, and lie limp on the tiled floor. Sally makes no remark, standing outside in the hall.

"I don't suppose you brought anything, clotheswise," she says. " 'Course not. I'll find an ensemble for you."

"From where?"

But she's already gone.

I step into the stall. There are round yellow splotches on the ceiling. Some slow-growing mold. The water, when it comes out, is rusty. At first it bounces off me, beads on my skin. I'm impermeable from the dirt and sweat of the last few days. Then gradually, with a stony bar of soap, I begin to clean myself.

"Your dad was a spiffy dresser," she calls.

"Will I fit in those?" I wipe a hole in the steamy glass long enough to see her hold up a pair of black pants.

"Don't see why not," her voice comes back. "Looks like your size. Hope you don't mind boxer shorts."

"No."

"Finish up, will you? I'm not dressed for a steam room. And don't forget about your hair."

Her arm appears with a bottle of shampoo. I take it, but take her hand too. Hold it.

"Allen," she says, her head appearing where the door is open just a crack. Steam rushes out. "Let go."

"I thought you were here to apologize."

"Well, not now."

"Why not?"

"All right." She squints through the drizzling water at my face. "I didn't mean to upset you about your dad."

"It's not true."

"You told me already and I believe you."

"Do you?"

"I don't care really," she shrugs. "About what he did or didn't do. He was just this sad man who lived next door. I'm sorry he hurt himself, but it's you I'm concerned about."

"Me? Why?"

"Because you're just sleepwalking through this."

"I am?"

"That's how it looks from the outside. I mean, they

find your dad in a tub of blood and you got this expression like, What's for dinner?"

"How am I supposed to act?"

"I don't know. More wild, I guess. Do something. Scream out loud. Punch a wall. That might help."

"Help how? Why do I need help?"

She doesn't answer.

"Do you know something, Sally?"

"I know lots." Her eyes, trying to avoid mine, dip down and then pop up again.

"What do you know?"

"I know trouble when it's staring me right in the face."

I pull her into the shower. The water tamps down the curls of her hair. They remind me of a field after a heavy rain. I unbutton her blouse. She kisses my fingers one at a time, then places my hand under her breast and pushes hard. I pin her to the shower wall. We kiss and sink lower, the water bathing us both now, making strange sounds as it bounces against the metal trim at the bottom of the glass door.

"Now you're just not listening to me," she murmurs, her eyes closed, a line of water making black eye shadow run down her cheek.

"Don't you want this to happen?"

"Oh I want it to. That's not the question."

"What is?"

"You. You're the big question mark around here." She won't let me go further. The shampoo has fallen down to the floor with us. She cleans my hair, working the thick liquid until foam is running down my back and over my forehead, into my eyes.

"What is it about this place?" I ask again.

I take the soap and wash off her face. We're getting up, clinging to each other because the floor is slippery. When we emerge, her clothes are plastered to her skin. She slaps at me when I try to help.

"You'll just damage something. Where can I get changed?"

"Changed to what?"

"To a princess, Einstein." She kisses me. "Where can I get dry clothes? Can't just run next door, you know."

"There are no women's clothes," I say. "He threw them all away when my mother died. There's Melissa's room, but—"

"Lucky I've kept my girlish figure." She steps out into the hallway. "Which one is it? Here?"

"Sally, don't."

"Why not?"

I stop her.

"I don't want to catch a summer cold," she says. "They're the worst."

"You can't go in there."

"Is that so?"

My naked arm is barring the door. She lifts it and slips past. I go in after her.

"Looks like someone's been," she observes.

Drawers are pulled out. A corner of the carpet is folded over. The closet door is open. Melissa's room, with its deep green carpet, many shades in a jungle pattern, evergreen fronds and spring green speckles, bands of verdigris and turquoise, is a ransacked shrine. Books are spilled along the shelves where they once stood. Even the bed has been stripped and clumsily reassembled.

"The police," I say, sitting down on the springy mattress.

"What a great job that must be." She gives herself a quick appraising look in the closet mirror. "You get to snoop, ask all sorts of personal questions."

Contrary to her modesty in the bathroom, now she walks naked over the thick carpet without any embarrassment.

"Oh that's OK," she says, noticing me. "You can stare. I've been naked in front of thirteen doctors. I mean really naked, you know? Spreadeagled."

"What for?"

"An operation. Well, a procedure, that's what they call it. They look around inside me, see what's the matter. Try and explain my infertility."

She bends over a drawer. It's the one Anderson referred to, full of underwear and stockings.

"Who wore all this?"

"Not my sister, apparently."

"I should think not." She holds up another pair of high-cut lace panties. "You know who would go wild for these?"

"Who?"

"Bob Bates, my husband. Mind if I try them on?"

I shrug as she steps into them.

"Just my size. Well, that's comforting."

"Why can't you have children, Sally?"

"There's evidence of a trauma." She models them in the mirror, turning this way and that. "You think I'm sexy?"

"Trauma?"

"That's the medical term. There's scarring on my tubes. Those eggs can't get past the rough spot in the road. Or if they do, they're damaged. Doctor said I must have had some illness when I was growing up. Measles or pneumonia or something, and those bumps are what's left over from the infection. But I don't remember anything."

"Maybe it happened when you were little. Did you ask your parents?"

"I don't ask nobody nothing," she says. "Except for you. You, I asked if I was sexy. And you didn't answer." She stays glued to her reflection. "So what happened to your sister, anyway?"

"She didn't come home from school one day. Simple as that."

"How old was she?"

"Fifteen."

"And what did your family do?"

"Nothing."

"Nothing?"

"What could we do? The police looked for her. The FBI came. Her picture was in the paper."

"That's all?"

"We waited."

"And what about you?"

"Me?" I look at her. "I waited too."

"Might explain why you seem just a tad distant sometimes. So you think I can have these?"

"Why not?"

"Bob will be so pleased."

spLit-LEVELs

She comes over and kisses me. I lie back.

"Of course there's always the possibility that Bob's sperm are what the medical people call lackluster," she breathes in my ear. "See, they might not have certain mountain-climbing skills which would help them get over that rough spot I told you about."

"Is that why you sleep with other men?" I ask. "Are you hoping they'll give you a child?"

"Of course. It's the only moral reason for adultery. I'm a very moral person, you know. They teach you that in the army."

"What about just now? In the shower? Was that an act?"

"Oh, Allen," she sighs. "Don't you see? We're two people going in different directions. I aspire to stability. This place is a refuge to me. My job is to hunker down. To do that, I need a kid. You, you're going backward here. Your job is to move on. We're just intersecting."

"This place is a refuge to you? From what?"

"What went before," she says. "My life. America."

Someone coughs.

Anderson and Wertz are standing at the door.

"Hello, Allen."

Anderson tries nodding at Sally too, but without looking. Wertz, though, is on tiptoe, peering over the taller man's shoulder. I'm half-dressed. I sit on the edge of the bed blocking their view, expecting Sally to squirrel under the covers. Instead, I feel a heavy bounce as she stands up wearing nothing but the flimsy briefs.

"Close your eyes," she orders.

They both do. At the door, armed now with a skirt and

92

blouse from Melissa's dresser, she pauses, blocked by Anderson, who just has his eyes closed, and Wertz, who covers his with both hands like a child.

"Awfully sorry," Anderson says blindly. "We tried the doorbell. Didn't think anyone was home. I thought you never came in here, Allen."

"Looks like he was just about to," Wertz grins.

It happens fast. Sally seems to turn away but at the same time kicks back. Her heel disappears between Wertz's legs. He lets out such a scream Anderson opens his eyes and whirls around, reaching for his gun. But she's already padding down the hall, her naked back to them, on her way to the bathroom.

"*Son of a bitch!*" Wertz yells, sinking slowly to the floor.

"Easy, easy." Anderson bends over him. "Let me see."

"Leave me alone." He turns to her. "You! You're under arrest."

"Easy," Anderson says again.

"She was in the army," I explain.

"Arrest her!"

"What for?"

"She assaulted me."

"We don't have time for this." Anderson helps Wertz to his feet. "Besides, I didn't see nothing. I had my eyes closed. I'm sure the lady just slipped."

"Slipped? She—"

"Allen, did you see anything?"

"See what?"

"Bastard," Wertz snarls.

"If you really want to make an issue out of this, Sergeant, then we got to go right off and get pictures taken."

"Pictures?" You can see the change come over Wertz's face, very slowly. One side is still angry while the other is wary, puzzled. "Pictures of what?"

"The area of assault," Anderson goes on. "Going to be all healed by the time of the trial. Got to have some nice eight-by-ten color glossies for the judge."

"Judge? Forget it." He gingerly pushes at his pants. "I don't want to see nothing. I'm not even going to look down there, the next few days."

"Just as well," Sally says, reentering the room briskly. Wertz jumps out of her way like she has an electric cattle prod. "You'll be pissing tomato juice for a week, anyway."

"Bitch."

"Me?" she asks. She's wearing a white skirt and a floral top.

"Time out." Anderson, like a harried referee, actually makes the T-sign with his hands. "Just everyone shut up, will they?"

"Why are you here?" she asks, ignoring his request. "You come barging in like a couple of rejects from 'Dragnet.' Can't you see what kind of state Allen's in?"

"Looked like he was doing OK to me," Wertz says, and takes an involuntary step back so his waist is behind a table.

"We're investigating a homicide," Anderson answers. "Now, Allen, is it possible we could speak to you?"

"Go ahead."

"Privately, I mean."

"Homicide?" She looks at me. "What are they talking

about?"

"A mistake."

"It's no mistake," Anderson says. "That blood we found on the ceiling? It's your dad's type all right."

"See? I told you."

"But it wasn't your dad who drew those letters."

"What do you mean?"

"Fingerprints. At the end of each stroke, the fingertip came to a rest. Left a partial impression. Enough to tell us that it's not your father's."

"Whose is it, then?"

"If I knew that . . ."

"Hey, look."

Wertz is kneeling on the floor.

"Is it there?" Anderson asks, unsurprised.

"Bingo." He pulls back the green carpet, the foam rubber cushion, and holds up a checked handkerchief.

"It looks like mine," I say, staring. "But I don't understand how it got there."

"Allen, honey, you shouldn't even be talking to these bozos," Sally warns. "Not alone, anyway."

"It was in my back pocket when I came out here," I go on, feeling for it. But of course I'm wearing my father's clothes now.

"She's right, you know." Anderson frowns. "Might be easier on everybody if you kept still."

Wertz has been examining it.

"Here," he announces. "On the corner, see? Just like she said."

"She?" I ask. "Who?"

Anderson shoots him a look. Wertz holds up the material and points to a dark patch.

"Tried to wash it off," he says, again to Anderson, ignoring me.

"Tried to wash what off?"

"There are tests," Anderson explains. "For blood. We'll have to take this into our lab. I wonder if you'd come too, Allen."

"Come where?"

"To the station with us. There are some questions we could ask you there. It's more official."

"Don't go, Allen," Sally says, getting up. "He is not your friend."

"He doesn't really have a whole lot of choice," Wertz says. "And if you make one more move, lady, I'm going to yell so loud . . ."

Anderson kneels to face me. Our eyes meet. His are sad and bloodshot.

"Are you arresting me?" I ask.

He hesitates.

"No. But I don't see why you won't cooperate, unless—"

"If you don't arrest me then I'm not coming with you."

He shakes his head and stands up.

"You planning any sudden departures, Allen?"

"My father's funeral is tomorrow," I remind him.

"I know." He turns to Sally. "Miss Bates, before you help this man in any way, I'd advise you to acquaint yourself with the legal definition of After the Fact."

"It's Mrs. Bates," she shoots back, but blushes when, on his way out, he looks over the mussed-up bed.

• • •

96

She was naked but wore red, one of those contradictions dreams contain so simply. I followed the chain with my teeth, letting its tiny links slide over the enamel, discovering between her breasts a gold cross.

"Where are you?" I asked.

"I'm right here." She hoisted herself higher to look past my shoulder. "I've been right here the whole time. It's everyone else who went away."

"I know. I'm as old as you now."

"Look," she said. "Look at the beautiful lawn."

We weren't speaking. The words were forming between us, a product of the shapes we made.

"I love it here," she went on. "I love the green."

"Allen?"

My eyes were already open. Somehow I blinked and woke again.

"Allen?" my mother called, standing unsteadily at the door to the garage. "Are you in here?"

I sat up, rolled down the window.

"Where's Dad?"

"Out." She held a tall glass of diet cream soda, at least a quarter of which was gin. A shapeless dress made her face hover, smile weakly at me, before she obliterated it with a cigarette. Her hair swept down over one eye like an old-time movie star's. "He hates that, you know."

"What?"

"You sleeping in the car."

"I wasn't sleeping."

"What were you doing then?"

"Thinking."

She nodded, looking for a place to tap her ash. She had

the whole floor of the garage, the oil-stained gasoline-reeking concrete pad, but instead daintily lifted a garbage can lid and used that.

"Do you know where he is?" I asked.

"No." For a moment she let herself be entranced by whatever was in the can, a banana skin, coffee grounds, then she snapped out of it and replaced the lid. "You should be out with your little friends, shouldn't you?"

"It's after eleven."

"Then you should be in bed."

Sacks softened the line of the wall. Fertilizer, sand, peat. Above them tools hung off a square of pegboard, each outlined in black marker so it could be put back in the right place. The shovel, I noticed, was missing, its empty representation fitting neatly between the rake and trowel. So he was out by the reservoir again, digging at random spots, walking with the delicate blade poised in front of him like a divining rod. I no longer went with him. I had asserted myself to that extent. Instead, I lay here. A crash of ice brought me back to the thick air of the garage as my mother finished her drink. She braced herself against the door frame. I searched her face for any sign of Melissa. But it had long since become an expressionless mask. The flesh hung loosely, like the folds of her dress below. Her lips made a sound, unsticking themselves from the cigarette filter. I could hear him shovelling, hitting a rock, that sickening clang, trying to pry it out, the steel shrieking over stone.

"How did you meet?"

"Meet?"

"You and Dad, I mean."

She was at that stage of drunkenness where she responded very slowly. Sometimes she would stay frozen until the cigarette burned down and singed her back to reality. Now she only smiled and regarded her empty glass with a look of betrayal.

"Friends," she answered. "When we were in school. Who knew each of us. Thought we'd hit it off."

"A blind date?"

"Shouldn't you be outside playing?"

"I'm too old to play."

"I know."

Turning, she blew a stream of smoke. I lay back down in the seat of the car. The dream of Melissa had left my body overwhelmed with sensation. Paralyzed.

On TV there are reruns. I've come back in time to catch the echoes of what I grew up to. In the comedies that dead studio laughter could be my own. Cops and robbers. Quiz shows. I followed TV as if learning something step by step. How to act. How to think. I catch a shallow glimpse of myself in the dusty glass, a child's watchful gaze.

My stomach, though, demands more to soothe the waves of panic. I can't face the freezer again, with my mother's handwriting on all the little corpses, the bare metal shelf my flesh sticks to if I linger too long. Outside, the night is warm and breezy. I drive to the McDonald's. It stands on the far edge of a traffic circle, near nothing except its own massive parking lot. I can't change lanes fast enough and go around again and again, fighting centrifugal force, gripping the wheel. The

Golden Arches approach and recede. Finally I make it through to the other side, park at the end of the lot, where green dumpsters line the return to forest, and walk a long way over asphalt.

"Hey, Mr. S." A car pulls up and cuts me off. "Don't go in there. There's a line."

"Are you following me, George?"

His face, reflected in the dashboard's glow, pretends to be baffled.

"Following you? No, we were just hanging out."

"We?"

Then I notice the cat's eyes of his girl again, with her arm proprietorially around the boy's waist.

"We saw you get out of your car. How come you park so far away?"

"I like to walk."

"Oh."

They both regard me as if I'm crazy.

"This is Nina," he says.

"Hello, Nina."

Her mouth moves but nothing comes out. She's eating a french fry. The whole car, in fact, as I lean in to talk with them, reeks of grease.

"You got to wait five, ten minutes in there, this time of night," he tells me. "And there's no place to sit."

"But I'm hungry."

"Well, hop in. We'll do the drive-thru."

"That's all right. I don't want to disturb you."

"Huh?"

The girl reaches for another french fry. She seems to

be plucking them out of his groin. That's where all the food is, a garbage dump spreading over his lap.

"George likes you," she says sulkily, and pops it into her mouth.

"Yeah." He nods. She has just translated some complicated sentiment. "Come on in."

It's a two-door. I walk around to the other side. Nina shrinks into her boyfriend, as if I took up much more space than I do.

"This is very nice of you."

He blasts the car off in a screeching orbit to line us up with the drive-thru window. I try clutching the door handle but it's all electronic. There's no place to hold on.

"I said to Nina"—he reaches down for a hamburger while heading directly for a brick wall—"that's Mr. Stanley's son. But she said it couldn't be."

"Why did you say that, Nina?"

I can't see her too well but I feel her resentment.

"I don't know," she mumbles. " 'Cause I thought you were someone else."

"Who?"

George laughs.

"Tell him."

She mumbles again, mostly into his shirt.

"What?"

"Nothing."

She leans down. A horrible death rattle comes out of George's chest. I can see, as my pupils open wider to collect more light, a straw sticking out. He's got his soda there, buttoned in place. Nina sucks at the ice.

"She thought you were your dad," George says, amused.

"But my father was old."

"Welcome to McDonald's," an amplified voice blares into the car. "May I help you?"

"Where's the menu?" I look around.

"Menu?" That, of all things, rouses the girl from her lethargy. "There's no menu."

"Quarter-Pounder with cheese, Coke, and fries?" George calls, looking to me for confirmation. "You want a shake?"

"No."

"And two more chocolate shakes."

"This is my favorite part," Nina says, straightening up in the seat, brushing crumbs of food off her shirt.

"What is?"

"Waiting."

I can see her better now. She's Polynesian-looking, inky Oriental hair, but wide and plump, with sturdy legs emerging from loose shorts. A dream of the South Seas, in suburbia.

"Let me," I say, when it comes time to pay.

We drive off, slowly now, Nina shifting as George steers and hollows his cheeks around his straw, trying to raise the impossibly thick brown sludge.

"You thought I was my father?"

"I forgot he was dead," she says. "You look just like him. The way you walk and the way you dress."

"These are his clothes."

"Yeah?"

"Did you know my father?"

102

"Not really. But George had a major crush on him."

"Shut up," he says fondly, tooling alongside the dumpsters now, just for the sake of motion. The parking lot is like a little city.

"Your dad talked to him. Nobody else does that. George's father just yells."

"He was a cool dude, all right," George nods. "He gave me advice."

"Like what?" I ask.

That puzzles him. He brakes the car, in no particular place, rolls down the window, and spits once over the side.

"Some weird shit in this shake."

"Gross," Nina says, and lifts off her own lid to investigate.

"Well, once he told me that no matter what I do I should make sure I marry a woman who's smarter than I am."

"It's cancer lumps," she frowns, poking at the surface of the shake with her straw. "This shake has cancer."

I take a big chomp, try to get everything in one bite, the pickle, the meat, the cheese, the bun, the mustard, the ketchup, even the waxy smell of the wrapping paper it comes in.

"I got to go to the girls' room," Nina says, tossing her half-drunk shake out onto the pavement.

"I'll drive you."

"No. That's OK."

She works her way over his lap to the car door.

"You sure? It's a long way."

"Oh, I like to walk," she says, imitating me.

They both laugh. She goes out and stays in the beam of the headlights. Her shorts are made of terrycloth. We watch her smooth dark thighs rub against the fuzzy fabric.

"You heard that joke about Oriental women?" George asks.

He takes one of my fries and dunks it in his shake.

"No."

"They say it's in sideways."

"What is?"

"It. You know. Like their eyes. That's why they can't slide down the bannister." He acts it out with his french fry. "They go boing! boing! boing! Like that. Anyway, it's not really true, in case you were wondering."

"So you've slept with her."

"Oh yeah."

"That's nice."

He seems to feel he has broken the ice.

"You know, I saw the girl."

"What girl."

"The one your dad was doing it with."

The beams illuminate blackness, tunnels of it, with more blackness on either side. There's an exhaust leak somewhere in the car, or maybe it's just fumes from the highway making me sick.

"Where did you see them?"

"At your house. In the window over the garage."

"Melissa's room?"

"Who's Melissa?"

"Never mind. What were you doing there?"

"I was just on the street," he says. "Nina lives down the

road from you. I was coming home after dropping her off and there were these funny shadows."

"You mean silhouettes?"

"Yeah," he brightens. "I guess."

"What did you see, George?"

"I told you: him and the girl. She had long hair. They were, you know, kissing." He says it with disgust. "Just for a minute. And then the light went off."

"Why didn't you tell me before, when I asked if you'd seen anyone?"

"We weren't alone then," he points out. "I don't want to get Nina freaked."

"Nina? Why would she be upset?"

"Well, living down the road from a pervert, you know. She's sensitive."

I pop the last bit of meat into my mouth. It's a way to avoid answering. He must have the same idea because he goes back to guzzling his shake, cancer lumps and all, putting his mouth to the rim, tilting back and bopping the bottom of the cup with his palm.

"This is what I've been trying to tell you," he says. "It's why I've been sort of keeping an eye on you."

"Did you ever see the girl?"

"You mean her face? No. But she had a great . . . what do you call it? Silhouette?"

"So you believe it too, what they say about him."

"I don't give a shit," he says stubbornly. "He was nice to me." He turns. "I was reading this nature magazine in a doctor's office, all about monkeys, how they have two brains."

"Two brains?" I echo, feeling slow.

"One in their head and then one in back that controls their tail."

"Oh. A ganglion. A cluster of nerves."

"Yeah. Well, I was thinking maybe we all have the same thing, you know? A separate brain . . . but for our dicks. That would explain about your dad, wouldn't it?"

"I think that's just . . . our brain, George."

"Yeah?"

"Hey," Nina says, appearing out of nowhere. "There's a guy looking at your car."

"Who?"

"I don't know. He's lying almost under it. But not like he's stealing it."

I get out.

"Don't you want me to drive you?"

"That's all right. I'll walk," I call. "Thanks, George."

"Thanks for the shake," he says, with his face back inside the container. "See you tomorrow."

"Tomorrow?"

"For the funeral."

"Oh. Yes."

His car light winks out as the door closes and I am lost, completely in the dark with no points of reference, a walker in a parking lot. I stand still, waiting for my eyes to adjust. Slowly the reflective lines appear, a grid I can use to orient myself. I take blind steps forward. There's no sound except the constant sea-murmur of traffic. Who put these parking lots here? That's what I want to know. From the air they must be the most conspicuous landmark of the suburbs, perfectly square or rectangular, with pagan patterns of decoration etched into them. I put my hands up just in time to avoid crashing into the metal dumpster. That means I'm at the border. I step over the edge, feel my feet sink into the cushiony earth, and drop my pants. A long piss into the scrub by the highway relieves my anxiety. I set off again, able to see more, and come to my car, where there is indeed a man underneath, only his torso and legs visible.

"Who's that?" he calls.

"The owner," I answer.

"Oh, good." The left foot waggles. "That's a warrant there. It gives me the right to search this vehicle."

The piece of paper is held down by a wrench. I can't read it in the light.

"I'm Forensic," he says, emerging now from under the front of the car. "Remember me?"

"Of course."

He holds up his greasy hands to indicate we can't shake.

"What are you doing here?" I ask.

"I told you." I follow his gaze to my hand, where I'm still holding the wrench, in a clenched fist. "That warrant gives me the right—"

"I mean, how did you know I was here?"

"Oh. We just knew."

"Then I'm being followed."

"I need that wrench," he nods. "It's police property."

"What's in the bag?" I point with the heavy tool to a Ziploc bag he's holding.

"This?" He holds it up. "Splinters."

"From where?"

"From your fender. You had a bit of an accident, it looks like."

I nod.

"The wrench," he says again. "I really have to be going now."

He's nervous, sweating.

"You need a ride?" I ask.

"No, I parked . . . closer to civilization." He gives a tight laugh and motions in the direction of the McDonald's. "Well . . ."

He passes by me and grabs the wrench. I let him take it. His footsteps go rapidly off, afraid. Afraid of me? I kneel where he was, by the car's front fender, and run my hands over the dent Pam made when she plowed us into that young tree. I feel the chrome tenderly, as if it was the bump on her forehead.

The traffic circle isn't as hard to handle, coming home. No headlights follow me up the last stretch of Oakdale Drive. Getting out of the car, I look up to the window George spoke of. But of course there's nothing, no month-old shadows of whatever happened here.

The house has been searched. They must have come back just after I left. Rugs turned up, books taken down, records out of their jackets. I walk through the bomb wreck of everything, kick objects gently out of my path, heading where? Just to keep walking is all I want. Finally there's the bedroom. The huge mattress has been tipped over and lies at an angle against the box spring. Even the clock has been taken down and sits with its face to the wall. Only the bathroom, which they already searched days ago, is the same as when I left. The stain still lies at the bottom of the tub. I get a bucket and some cleanser, strip, and step into the middle of it all. I have this flash of fear the water will rehydrate the whole bloody scene like in a horror movie. But no. Each wipe just reveals more clean glassy porcelain. Naked, I scrub for at least an hour, until all traces are gone. Then I lie back and turn on the faucets. Clean water splashes around my ankles, my ears. That warm moment comes when my body goes weightless and slowly floats off the bottom of the tub. I drift into an echoey, aqueous silence.

chapter 5

UP HERE, EVERYTHING looks like its own map, the land all parcelled out, bordered, the road running through it. Shingles overlap and extend away. I am on the roof, level with the treetops, green shoots and tender young acorns just beyond my reach. Since the development never grew but was *conceived*, it should be knowable, simply the structure of a developer's brain as embodied in the houses he built, the roads he laid out. But I can't seem to penetrate the depthless facade. Instead I feel myself succumbing to it, just a plastic figurine set down on an architectural model to give it scale.

"Corky!"

Playmore squints, as if I'm invisible. He's all in black, wearing a strange Edwardian-looking frock coat with big buttons. Black shoes too, and a black hearse behind him, parked by the curb.

111

"Are you all right, Allen?"

"I'm fine. What are you doing here?"

"It's part of the package," he says tonelessly. "Didn't you read the brochure?"

"You mean I paid for all this?"

"Door-to-door service."

"Is he in back there?"

"No, of course not." He puts his hands on his hips. "Didn't you read the timetable I gave you?"

"I saw something about food, but—"

"The reception is in the Gold Package. You didn't pay for that. Yours is the Basic Plan. Viewing, service, interment." He shakes his head. "Have you been drinking?"

"No."

"Then what are you doing on the roof?"

"If I could only get higher," I mumble.

"What?"

"I'm just trying to make sense of things."

"Don't bother," he advises. "Come down or we'll be late."

"They can't start without us, can they?"

"No. I suppose not."

"Corky, you said something before, about how it was when your father died."

He looks up and down the street, embarrassed to be talking across such a gap, having to pitch his voice.

"I told you it was difficult. Technically. I had to charge extra."

"Charge who?"

"Myself."

"That's not what I meant. You said it was . . . liberating."

112

He nods, staring up at me, looking more than ever like he did twenty years ago, a wise child, that solemn adoring gaze.

"It made me feel alive," he says. "It made me feel everything I did mattered now."

"Didn't it matter before?"

"Not in the same way. Suddenly your actions exist. Exist in time." He shrugs. "It's impossible to explain. You don't feel it?"

"No."

"Maybe because you haven't buried him yet."

The hearse barrels down empty streets, rolling like a badly loaded ship.

"I was up all night with your father," Corky goes on.

"That's nice."

"He had an enormous penis, did you know that?"

"No. I didn't."

It's not the kind of day with a sunrise, just a suffused, cloudy increase in light.

"You're alone?" he asks quietly.

"That woman I came to see you with wasn't really my wife."

"Oh, I know." He pushes in the cigarette lighter. "I was just having fun."

"You know who she is?"

"Well, I've seen her. I know most of what goes on in this place."

"What do you know about my father?"

"I just told you, didn't I?" He takes a joint out of his coat pocket. "Want some?"

"No."

"I think you should." He lights the marijuana and takes a hit himself, letting the hearse wander all over the road.

"Why?"

"Because I know what's in store for you, Allen. And it's not pleasant. Believe me."

The last phrase is in a high, tucked-back voice. His lungs are otherwise occupied. I hold the joint and consider it while Corky straightens out our course and blows a long shaft of green smoke.

"Are you talking about my father? What they say about him and Melissa?"

"How did that rumor ever get started?" he wonders.

"People will believe anything."

"There must have been some basis in fact, don't you think?"

I shake my head.

"Are you going to have that?" he asks.

Out of politeness I take a hit. He retrieves the joint and once more loses control of the vehicle. The dotted white line is directly in front of me, hurling short choppy spears into my chest. I tear my vision away and focus on the rich fabric of his coat, the liver spots of his almost webbed hands.

"You should have seen their faces," I try explaining. "How easily they believed it. They would have believed anything about him. Just because he was different, because he read books and knew Greek, because he wore vests and string ties. The sad part is all he wanted to do was fit in, be one of them. He just didn't know how."

"Still," Corky argues, "he was acting strange, wasn't he? I hear people saw him afterward—"

"Nothing happened here," I insist. "Why are you bringing this up, especially now? Today, I mean."

"Oh, Allen." He flicks the joint out the window as we come to the funeral home. "Why do you think?"

The hearse strains, trying to make it up the steep grade of the drive. He parks us in front of the big, white-columned porch. It looks, I notice for the first time, like a Southern mansion, something out of *Gone With the Wind*.

"How much do you remember?" he asks, not moving to get out.

"Remember?"

"About here. What happened here when we were kids."

"Not a lot."

"But you remembered me. As soon as I opened the door."

"You'd be hard to forget."

"Do you remember what happened to me?"

"Of course."

He smiles.

"Those boys who held me down? Who chopped off my hair?"

"I remember."

He runs his hands through the thinning, lifeless strands that remain.

"It grew down to my waist, you know. Everyone used to look at me. I was the first. Even you—" He stops. "You came up to me one day and asked me how it felt, to have hair so long. And I said it was breezy, and that when the wind blew I felt like I was going to float away."

I stare with him past the funeral home's idyllic green lawn, past the supermarket and the parking lot, to the buzzsaw edge of the highway. A group of people are coming out of the liquor store.

"I remember," I say again.

"You said I looked beautiful."

"Did I?"

"They're asking questions," he finally answers. "About all the old rumors. About your father and Melissa. About everything. I thought if you knew first. If you were prepared—"

"I've got nothing to hide," I say automatically, getting out of the hearse.

"Allen, people say he—"

"I know you care, Corky. I know you're trying to help. But don't say any more. All right?"

"I'm just watching out for your ass," he sighs. "Same as always."

"We've been having a good old-fashioned wake," Sally explains, holding up the hem of her skirt like a pioneer lady, as she negotiates the hill. "Johnny even closed the bar to come over."

"Out of respect," the fat man says.

"Bob Bates." Sally's husband sticks out his hand, holding himself stiffly erect. He's so short I can see the pattern on the top of his scalp, the dark black hair and bright white skin.

"Pleased to meet you," I say.

His grip is like a bear trap.

"Nasty business," he complains.

"What is?"

"Your father." He nods to the portico door. "You believe in God?"

"Now, Bob," Sally yawns, staggering as she closes her eyes. The fat man obligingly grips her elbow. "Allen here is in the process of mourning. Can't you see that?"

"We should go in," Playmore says. "I'll prepare the chapel."

"Chapel?"

"Don't worry," he smiles. "It's nondenominational."

"What has it got, posters of football players?" Sally calls after him.

She's drunk, of course. But aggressively, edgily drunk. The most upset.

"You can't do anything until you decide if you believe in God or not," Bob Bates insists, literally standing his ground, his arms crossed in front of his chest, daring the world to knock him over. A military bearing. I remember Sally saying how they met in the army.

"I don't believe in God," Johnny unexpectedly volunteers. "I have a theory that accounts for life much better. What if the world is really run by—"

"—We didn't know your father too well," Bob interrupts.

"Hardly at all," Sally adds.

"What you must remember is that even he was created in God's image."

"Ain't that a kick?"

"Do you find yourself subject to temptation?" Bob asks suspiciously.

"Temptation?"

"These tendencies do run in the family sometimes."

"Bob!" Sally warns.

Anderson and Wertz come. Anderson shakes my hand but doesn't say anything. Wertz nods and hangs back, looks disapprovingly at Sally. George appears from around the side of the funeral home. He's wearing a tight black T-shirt and a headband to keep stray blond hairs out of his face.

"Hey, Mr. S. Sorry Nina couldn't come. She's not feeling too good."

"Where's your car?" I ask, surprisingly moved to see him.

"I left it," he says. "Thought I'd walk."

"You walked?"

"Yeah, well I thought I would think of him more if I walked, you know? Nothing else to do. Took me almost an hour."

He grins down at his sneakers.

"Is this all?" Corky asks, poking his head out the door and counting silently, moving his lips.

Presidents line the walls of Corky's chapel. Eisenhower, Kennedy, Nixon, Reagan, large iconic airbrushed photo-portraits looming over the plush red carpet and black altar where the coffin is laid.

"We're all Americans," he explains. "That's what I meant by nondenominational."

"It's tasteful," Sally says, her hands twisting against a small purse, surveying the sides of the room so she approaches the coffin indirectly.

"Sneaking up on him." Johnny, standing next to me,

smiles good-naturedly. "Scared your old man might give her the evil eye."

Corky takes my arm. There are rows of folding chairs with a central aisle, the coffin at the end of it. We progress slowly. He pauses between steps.

"Go slow," he counsels. "Think of it as a wedding."

There's cheap organ music on a loop tape. By the time we get to the front row, I've heard the same tune twice. The face is puffy and pink, as it never was in real life. His lips are bee-stung, like Cupid or Bacchus in some Renaissance painting. His cheeks are plumped and rouged. The mouth not quite in a smile, more a tight, jaw-jutted clench, as if tensing for an injection.

"Wax." Corky nods down at the corpse proudly. "With that much blood loss I had to insert hot wax and then model the face like clay. That's probably how he looked when he was your age."

"Mr. Stanley?" George asks dubiously, talking to the body, not me.

"This is all very artistic," Sally decides, finally coming up to the coffin. She includes Corky's embalming job in the general praise of the room. "This would be a good place for Occasions."

"I do rent it out," he says. "Cub Scout meetings, the annual Boys Swim Team dinner, things like that."

"You have a private viewing room available too?" she wonders. "With a sofa maybe?"

"I have a room. But not with anything besides chairs . . . except the coffin, of course."

She puts her hand beside my father's head, tests the cushion.

"Soft," she says admiringly.

"I'd like to say a few words," Bob Bates announces.

Nobody else seems surprised.

"Bob's a lay preacher," Sally explains.

"Shall we sit?"

Corky herds us into rows, making sure he and I are in front. There's a window facing the parking lot. I can see Anderson outside, standing by his unmarked car with the police radio receiver stretched out the window. He's talking to someone very seriously, looking inside at the same time. I turn around. Wertz hasn't sat. He's standing in back, as if on guard duty.

"Poor bastard," Corky sighs, a prelude to any formal eulogy.

"Proverbs 26:11," Bob begins, standing at the lectern. " 'The fool returneth to his folly like the dog unto his vomit.' "

"Amen," Sally answers.

"My father was not a child molester," I say under my breath.

"Of course he wasn't," Corky assures me. "People here are so provincial. They think pedophilia and incest are the same thing."

"He wasn't that either!"

"What does it matter, Allen?" He turns to the lectern. "Everyone involved is dead now, except you."

"When I look around this room," Bates says, "and I see all these great men on the wall staring down at us, I think of Jesus at Gethsemane. What a great president he would have made."

"Jesus?" George asks involuntarily.

"Here in America, we are so alone. We are left only with our faith. And even that sometimes wavers. If you walk far enough in any direction you will come to wilderness, the same wilderness where Jesus was tempted by the Devil. And we too, all of us, are tempted every day of our lives. Tempted to give in to the nothingness we imagine surrounds us. Tempted to despair. Tempted to sin."

"But Jesus wasn't born here," George says, genuinely puzzled. "We were just studying that last year. To be president you have to—"

"I did not know the deceased well." Bob looks to the coffin. "And I can't say I'm sorry about that, having heard some unsavory details about his past. But I do know why his life ended so tragically. Because he had no leadership, no moral example to guide him. The values he took for granted were being corrupted. The world his community was built on seemed to be collapsing all around him. In the end, the Devil came and tempted him. What lesson can we learn from this man's life? That in times like these we must cling to our faith. We must search for Jesus. Because he is out there. His face has been seen. In billboards. On the back of milk cartons. Behind the blank screen of the TV. He is coming. Our savior. The answer to our prayers."

"What I don't understand," I ask, "is why they're all here."

"Who?"

"These people." I risk a look around. "If they all thought he was a . . ."

"Pervert," Corky supplies. "They're curious."

"Because he killed himself?"

"They're curious about you. You're new."

"I'm not new."

"You are to them. They haven't found out about you yet."

"Found out what?"

"Jesus wasn't old enough either," George mumbles behind us. "To be president you have to be at least thirty-five."

"Well, he'd be a lot older now," Sally points out.

"Let us pray for the soul of this man. But let us also pray for the soul of America."

Bob smiles maniacally. Corky straightens his suit, preparing to get up.

"Let us pray," Bob repeats, seeing him, and hops down off the podium, flexing his Popeye arms.

Corky lets the organ music play for a decent interval—nobody is actually praying—then wipes his forehead with a handkerchief.

"We will assemble in the parking lot in five minutes. The interment will be at Mount Gladeview. There will be no reception afterward."

"Drinks at my place," Johnny adds, half-rising from his seat to make the announcement. "If that's OK with you."

I shrug.

Outside, the cars rev up, the hearse in front, Corky orchestrating it all.

"Hey, who's going to give me a ride?" George calls. "The one time I don't bring my car. I didn't know there was going to be a parade."

"Procession," Corky corrects.

"You can ride with me," Johnny says, pointing to a yellow subcompact with a tattered vinyl roof.

"You drive that?"

"It's a Maverick," the fat man says defiantly. "What's wrong with a Maverick?"

"Nothing, I guess."

"You coming or not?"

The boy trots off after the fat man, down the hill.

"What about me?" I realize, looking over to Corky. "Do I ride with you again?"

"No," he says, giving me a sad look as he steps into the hearse.

"But then how do I get to the cemetery?"

"Us."

Anderson and Wertz are standing on either side of me.

"You get a police escort," Wertz says. "Lucky, huh?"

"Sorry I missed the service." Anderson pats my shoulder. "But some important information just came in."

"More information?"

"Got a lot of ground to cover, Allen." He leads me to the back seat. "And not much time."

"Allen," Corky calls mournfully. "My condolences."

Anderson stays in back with me while Wertz drives. The magnetic revolving police light is clapped on the roof.

"Sorry about your father," he begins.

"Thanks."

"Still time to tell us about it, you know."

"Tell you about what?"

"Slow down, will you? It's a funeral here," he calls.

Wertz nods. There is only the unmarked car, the

hearse, then Sally and Bob Bates, followed by Johnny and George. We crawl along the right-hand lane of the highway, well below the speed limit. Cars whiz by, some honking angrily.

"Why did you tear apart my house?" I remember. "What were you looking for?"

"Well, the razor blade. It is the murder weapon, after all."

"Oh."

"You know a place called the culvert, Allen?"

"What's that?"

"A necking spot," Wertz says from up front. "It's after our time. When we were in school, it was behind the Dairy Queen. Remember that?"

"No."

He rubs the bristles of hair on his sunburned neck.

"The culvert is a runoff ditch for a new development," Anderson goes on. "Kids hang out there, sit on the banks, drink, smoke pot, get carnal."

"Get carnal?" I echo, despite knowing I shouldn't say anything.

"We have a witness who places you at the culvert a week ago."

"Who?"

"That's confidential."

"She's wrong."

"She?"

"You said it was a woman who called, when you were at the house yesterday, remember? When you found my handkerchief."

Anderson nods.

124

"Where were you, Allen?"

"A week ago? In the city."

"Doing what?"

"When?" I ask. "What day?"

"Last Saturday."

"I was . . . How should I know what I was doing last Saturday?"

We're going by a fence, its rapidly shifting sections, all at slightly different heights, topped with a continuous curlicue of barbed wire.

"Think," he suggests. "Think hard."

"I was probably at home. Watching TV. Or eating Chinese food. I don't know."

"Sounds exciting," Wertz says. "You see anybody? You go out on a date?"

"No."

He shakes his head.

"That's too bad for you, Allen."

"Paint from your father's car matches some found on a small tree that was knocked down on the roadside by the culvert," Anderson continues quickly, as if this was something distasteful to get over with. "Apparently he was out there too. I can only imagine what he was doing. Maybe you can tell us."

"Kid goes to the necking place about twenty years too late," Wertz laughs. "Hey, remember this?"

He lets go of the steering wheel and with both hands does a mime of kissing someone from behind, where his own hands become a lover's, caressing his temples and shoulders. The car begins to veer.

"Don't be an asshole," Anderson snaps.

125

"Except you didn't kiss anyone," Wertz resumes, driving again. "You just watched."

It hangs in the air a moment.

"This is where we turn," Anderson says.

"I know."

He leads the procession off the highway, past a bowling alley and a movie sixplex.

"What do you want?" I finally get out.

"We want to know how your handkerchief got blood on it," Anderson says. "Same blood type as your father's."

"See, what we figure," Wertz summarizes, "is that you follow your father out to this ditch."

"Culvert," Anderson corrects.

"Whatever. And you spot him doing something there. Something that brings back memories. Maybe of what he did to your sister."

A truck stop goes by, then the gates to the cemetery. Wertz leads us all inside.

"So you go home, let yourself in with that extra key, and wait for him. He comes back. Maybe he decides to take a bath, maybe you force him down into the tub. Who knows? You take the razor blade and—"

"Five?" the guard at the entrance asks.

"The Stanley party!" Corky calls from behind us.

The guard nods, takes off his hat as we roll in.

"Some party, huh?" Wertz grins. I can see his healthy horseteeth in the mirror. "Where do we go now?"

"We can drive right up," Anderson says. "Just follow him."

The hearse goes on ahead, on a narrow road surrounded by grass and miniature mausoleums.

"Why?" I ask. "Why would I come back here in the first place?"

"You tell me," Wertz shrugs. "Maybe you got homesick."

"And how would I know about the culvert?"

"Maybe someone called you up, told you what was happening. Maybe you'd been back before."

Anderson clears his throat.

"I read those reports. The ones about Melissa's disappearance. Local police. State police. FBI. Did you know they had a suspect?"

I turn, look at him.

"Who?"

"Your father."

"They were wrong."

"The chronology he gave for his whereabouts during the disappearance doesn't make sense. There was time he couldn't account for."

"He was looking for her."

"So he said. Then there's your mother."

"What about my mother?"

"The accident. Truck driver said she rammed right into him. Didn't even slow down."

"That was years later."

"She had an alcohol count of point nineteen."

"She was . . . griefstricken."

"Where is this guy getting buried, anyway?" Wertz asks. "Nevada?"

"It's in the new section," Anderson answers. "Keep going."

"Great."

"And you were there," he says, putting his hand on my shoulder again. "You were in that house. You must have known. You're the only person left who knows what really happened."

"Nothing happened."

"It's so obvious. The man destroyed your life."

"What do you mean, destroyed? My life isn't over."

"My only question is: What took you so long? Why now, after all these years?"

His grip on my shoulder tightens. The car jerks to a sudden halt.

"Time to plant him," Wertz announces.

"This is wrong," I say, not moving.

Wertz, turning as he opens the door, seems to smile in agreement.

"Things don't always fit perfect at first. It's not an exact science. But once we get the basic idea right, everything else just falls into place. You'd be amazed."

"By the way," Anderson says. "You're under arrest. We just wanted to show you the common courtesy of letting you attend the funeral. Then you'll have to come back with us."

"I didn't kill him," I finally say.

"You can't even remember what you were doing last Saturday night," Anderson points out. "Maybe there's a reason you forget so much. Ever think of that?"

"Allen?" Sally sticks her face in. "Hurry up, hon. Bob's got to get some sleep before going to work."

A wind has come up, the first hint of fall. I open the door and climb out. The car seems deep. I grab its body, its frame, and haul myself up into the green grass, the blue sky, the hundreds of white and gray and pink tomb-stones. Everyone is standing by a piece of dark quilted cloth, several rows in. The coffin has been transferred to a dolly. Two workmen in dirty clothes wait along with the rest. I smile at them, look out over the endless vista of stones. There's nowhere to run. The procession of cars is confined to the narrow access road. Already another one is waiting for us to finish, its engine idling. Something shifts inside me, a piece of shipwreck jarred loose, floating up years later.

"Would you like to say a few words?" Corky asks.

"It's like a monk's room," my date said. I was disappointed she did not think of cell, a monk's cell, but plowed on with the obvious answer that she was crediting me with more restraint than I had. She frowned, didn't understand. Her hair had incredible curls, all held in place with spray. I nuzzled through them, swallowing the taste of plastic. My tongue went numb.

"Stop it." She shook her head.

"Stop what?"

"I don't know. What you're doing up there."

I put my ear to her abdomen, like a safecracker. Downstairs, far away but perfectly clear, came harpsichord music.

"Are you sure it's OK?" she asked nervously.

"I told you, he sleeps there all the time."

"Isn't he going to come up and go to bed?"

"No. That record just plays all night. The arm goes back."

In a golden net of sound he was splayed on the sofa.

We had tiptoed past, she lingering, staring.

"So that's him, huh?"

"Yes."

Being impotent was like reaching for and not finding my wallet. An eternity of panic and self-recrimination, all of which took ten minutes. It was still early. Only a cavity stretching from my Adam's apple to my knees suggested something odd might have happened. I led her quietly down the stairs. The needle, in the process of beginning again, skittered across the surface before finding the groove. My father mumbled in his sleep. One half of a conversation.

"I'm OK," she said.

"I'll take you home."

"No." She laid her open hand on my chest, forming a wall. "I told you, I'm OK."

I had closed the front door so carefully I did not feel it lock. But when I tried the knob again, outside now, after seeing her off, it was firm. I still heard the harpsichord music, so deeply had it sunk into my brain from years of sleeping to it, ever since my mother died, having it form the fabric of the nighttime air, each taut wire plucked, dry and perfect. I walked backwards, unsteady loping steps, trying to fit the whole house into my vision. Now, of course, I was hard. Excited by what? The grass underfoot? The prospect of leaving soon? I kept moving backwards to take it all in, as if I was a camera, unable to choose my subject, forced to focus only where I was pointed, where I was placed.

• • •

"No," I answer.

Corky, with a magician's flair, whisks aside the quilted cloth to reveal the hole. The workmen feed the shiny coffin down inside. Nobody says anything. And then he's gone.

"Well, that's that," Johnny says, looking at his watch. "I hope you didn't mind me making that announcement about drinks at my place."

"No. It was a very kind gesture."

"Business has been terrible lately," he confides. "I figure if I charge half-price, make it like Happy Hour—"

"That's fine."

"I'm afraid we won't be able to join you," Anderson says, taking me by the elbow again.

Wertz has a pair of handcuffs out.

"Are those necessary?"

"Regulations," he says. "Don't worry, after a while you won't even notice them."

Impatient, the last car in line comes careening past the nearest row of headstones. The three of us jump out of the way. It screeches to a halt right in front of me.

A woman in a high fur turban and dark glasses is driving.

The door swings open, knocking Anderson aside and catching Wertz in the groin.

"Jesus fucking Christ!" he screams.

"Get in," she says.

Before I can close it we're moving, sixty miles an hour easy, churning up turf and gravel, bouncing past graves, with the door still flapping.

"Close that, will you?"

We go racketing over the access road and then out the gate, the guard taking his hat off again as we pass. I'm vaguely aware of sounds behind us, a siren and horns.

"Allen?" she asks. "Are you OK?"

I pull at the leopardskin-patterned sweatshirt she has wrapped around her hair. It comes off and frees a long chestnut braid. She takes off the dark glasses herself.

"Finally got my Learner's Permit," she says.

"Happy Birthday, Pam."

"Silly. My birthday's not for three months."

She drives very well, not too nervous or reckless, just at the speed limit now.

"Whose car is this?"

"Uncle Steve's."

"You mean Wertz's?"

"Uh-huh." She guides it off the highway, into her own development. "He lives just down the road from us. He leaves the keys in the ignition."

"What are you going to do?"

"Return it, of course."

I look back. There's no one behind us.

"We can stay at home until dark," she goes on. "My mom and stepdad are both at work."

"Pam—" I look down at my hands. Absolutely solid, not trembling at all. But they have been gripping the edge of the seat for fifteen minutes. I try to unclench them, sending signal after signal to the adrenaline-locked joints.

"I heard him," she explains. "He was talking to that black man on the phone."

"Anderson."

132

"You should hear what he calls that guy," she giggles.

"What did your uncle say?"

"That they were going to arrest you after the funeral. That's why he was using the police car instead of his own."

She's made an attempt to dress like a grown-up, with a black blouse and cotton print pants. Even the braid, which heightens her cheekbones and forehead, is a young woman's, not a girl's.

"You should have called me," I say.

"Your phone is tapped," she answers. "They really think you did it. Did you?"

"Do what?"

"Kill your father?"

"No."

"Oh." She's disappointed. "Well, you have to get away anyway, because they really think you did."

Wertz's place is more like a bungalow, squeezed in at the end of the road, a cramped little box with a neighbor's fence on one side and woods on the other.

"Uncle Steve's a bachelor. That's why he spends so much time at our house."

"You're just going to leave the car here?"

"He won't be back for a while. He'll be looking for you, right?" She hops out and slams the door. "You like my braid?"

"It's nice."

I reach to run it through my hand like a string of pearls, but she ducks away.

"Don't! It took me forever to do."

"Aren't you scared?"

"Of what?"

133

"Stealing your uncle's car, for one thing. Don't you think he'll recognize it?"

"Uncle Steve is color-blind."

"But still—"

"Come on," she says. "Let's go to my house. Nobody will be back until late. Are you hungry?"

She seems so unconcerned, raising her arms and stretching as she walks, a sun worshipper or a sleeper after a long night. The shiny braid swings like a pendulum.

"At the culvert," I remember, "when you were holding on to me, you took a handkerchief out of my back pocket, didn't you?"

"Did I?"

"It turned up later, at my house, with blood on it."

"So you got it back. Good."

"Yes. No, actually. The police have it."

"They really hate you, you know. I wonder why."

"Because of my father."

"You do look like him."

"How do you know?" I ask. "How do you know what he looked like?"

"Here we are," she announces.

It's where I drove by before, dropping her off, an electric blue ranch-style house with a violently green lawn. One tree sprouts out of it, as if by magic, just a slit cut in the grass carpet. Around an island of shrubbery there are rich brown woodchips and a border of miniature rounded bricks.

"Don't step on the lawn." She skips on ahead of me. "Use the path."

I follow her on scattered flagstones, like dancing up a rocky stream. She takes out a key and leads me in.

"Well?" I demand, ignoring the vulgar decor, the Colonial motif. "How did you know what my father looked like?"

"I must have seen a picture," she smiles, locking the door, putting away the key.

"No."

"Well, maybe I just figured he looked like you. I mean, you wear his old clothes and drive his car, so—"

I reach behind and take the thick chestnut braid. I pull her hair back.

"Stop it," she says, pushing at me.

"I need to know what happened."

"You're hurting me."

"Were you sleeping with my father?"

"No!"

"But you knew him, didn't you?"

Her legs are kicking. I force her back against the wall. Then I glimpse, trying to catch her frightened eyes, a cut inside the open collar of her blouse. It's recent, a bloody, ugly wound, and goes all the way down between her breasts.

"Who did this to you?" I ask.

It's the last thing I remember.

chapter 6

SATURDAY NIGHT. HEIDI'S hair was cut so high you could see where her ears ended, their very tips, delicate and veiny. I ran my lips where it had been snipped away. Her skirt also ended quickly, until my hands, disoriented in the dark, weren't sure where they were, what they were touching. I imagined I was swimming through her, stretched out until my feet hooked over the bottom of the bed.

"No, seriously," she said, still chatting in a cocktail-party voice. "In Berlin I can go anywhere, at any hour, and there is always fun, and there is always friends."

"That's because Europe is an ant colony," I grunted.

I was looking for the right place to put my mouth. But it was so dark, like an air raid we were sitting out in each other's body.

"Europe is what?"

137

"An ant colony. Everyone's the same. Here in America—"

And then we found each other. I couldn't tell before if she'd been struggling or helping. Now I heard her mutter or sigh one long syllable that sounded almost Japanese.

"So-o-o . . ."

She was a professional, who would be on top. I could watch the beginning of her second chin, where the tiny residue of what her face had seen was collecting, a pouch, just its shadow, shaking slightly each time she rose and fell. Then she would walk away. That was part of it. I would watch her body, her spine, the cleft of her ass, then each leg, utterly animal and natural, on her way to the kitchenette to get coffee.

"Why do guys like it that way?" she asked.

"What way?"

"Like this."

She put my penis between her breasts.

"I don't like it that way," I said, looking up as far as I could from where I lay, frowning.

". . . weird of them," she went on, bouncing, maneuvering on the mattress, which was just a fold-out sofa. The smell of old, nicotine-infested cushions and bolsters was all around us.

She wasn't really German. That was an act. It was to give her an excuse for being there, that she was a foreign student and needed money. It's what she told the men at the bar so they wouldn't think she was a whore. "I am just, how do you say? A bar girl."

That first night, before I knew, I asked her all about Germany, nervous that she hadn't told me to leave. She smoked cigarettes and put them out in an old ice-cream dish by the side of the bed.

"Yes, in some ways it is better. But of course you don't have the freedom there."

"I want to owe you," I said. "I mean, I want to pay you."

"We can make this a regular thing, yes?"

And that's how it began. She dropped the accent later on, when we got to know each other. At least I'm paying my own way, I told myself. That made me feel better. I got to watch her from underneath with total removal, as if I were an anatomist. And when I went to the bar again and asked for her, they said she didn't work there anymore, that she'd found another source of income.

Me.

I spent hours staring at her forehead. It was perfectly empty, like the marble of a statue. I looked all through her cosmetics in the bathroom, for what I don't know. Some magic cream that explained how she could move me so much, yet be unreal at the same time, just a paid girl. I watched myself from the corner of the room, her walking across the rug, climbing up onto the bed, climbing up on top of me. The same motion.

"This is an almost dreamlike state you're describing," the doctor said.

"It's instead of dreaming that I go to her. I don't dream."

"Everyone dreams. You just don't remember your dreams."

"Same thing."

He was confined to a wheelchair. Not that he was in it.

He was in an armchair when I came in. The door had been open. But I glimpsed the wheelchair as I passed the little kitchen. And I noticed he never got up. A cane was by the side table. I sat across from him.

"I walk out the door. And I lock it behind me. And I turn around. And there's nowhere I want to go. I just stand out in the hallway. Then I turn around and go back in."

"You're depressed," he said.

"So how do I get undepressed?"

"It takes time."

". . . and a lot of money, right?"

He was putting on his glasses. His hands shook. What did he have? I wondered. He wrote me a few numbers and names.

"Unfortunately, I'm not taking on any new patients. These are some people I can recommend."

It was a nice apartment, with bric-a-brac and greenery all over the place. I didn't think you were supposed to see where psychiatrists lived. It was the first time I'd ever been to one. There was thick, old white lead paint, like frosting, on all the doors and window frames.

"But I like you. Couldn't you see me a few times?"

His glasses were on the end of his nose. He smiled. Then his hands were pressing against the arms of the chair, as if he was trying to get up, but he wasn't, he was just rigid all of a sudden.

"You OK?"

"No," he said, to something above or over my shoulder.

Whatever it was passed and he sat back, looking beyond me, out the window at the building opposite.

"I wonder if you'd mind phoning someone?"

"One of these guys?" I held up the sheet of notepaper he'd given me.

"No," he smiled. "A real doctor."

I found myself walking the streets all night, ending up downtown at dawn, dancing almost, picking my way over the cobblestones, trying to stay on top of these giant molars, and realized I was drunkenly weaving, inviting violence. But nobody stopped me. I felt the mist rushing off the stone landscape. That rare sense of being on the sea.

"You ever had sex in front of the TV?"

"No."

She sat facing me on propped knees.

"Isn't this going to be hard for you?" I asked, politely trying to look over her shoulder.

"How much was she asking?"

"Who?"

"That girl near the bus station. Darlene."

"How do you know her name was Darlene?"

"From where you met her. From what she said."

"I thought you never did that. On the street, I mean."

"I'm writing a book." That was her standard answer whenever I wondered why she knew certain things. "Lean back."

It was a deep wicker chair. It creaked with both our weights.

"Darlene's a man," she said.

We didn't fit too well, but she was right, it was incredibly erotic. When I got up, I felt the imprint of wicker all over my back. After she left, I went to the closet, flipped out the belly of the vacuum cleaner, and got more bills. I

141

stuck a hundred in my back pocket and went out, leaving the TV on like a watchdog.

"Darlene?" I asked into the night.

There was nobody on the corner.

"Darlene?"

But she or he had either quit for the night or picked someone up. I turned in a slow circle, letting chance choose my direction. It was a Saturday night. Last Saturday night.

"Darlene?"

Something is behind my head. I move to push it out of the way but it's part of me, a bump so tender the pain of touching it shocks me awake.

"I remember where I was!"

"Shhh," she says.

The smell of food. My eyes try adjusting to the black, only a crack of yellow light under the door. We are on a soft mattress, like a pit, with sickly down pillows and a scratchy blanket.

"They haven't gone to bed yet," Pam whispers.

"Who?"

"My parents. We have to be quiet."

We lie still, touching all along our sides. The room slowly appears: a cluttered dresser top, a nature poster on the wall, a closet so crammed with clothes the door doesn't shut.

"What's that smell?"

"Dinner. They got home late. It's past midnight."

I am still in my clothes. She is wearing only a large white T-shirt. It ends below her hips like a short dress.

From the hall comes the drone of the dishwasher.

"What happened?"

"You started acting like a jerk," she hisses.

"Where am I?"

"My room. Don't worry. We can get away as soon as they're asleep."

"Get away?"

"From the police! Remember?"

"Slow down." My head feels like some infinitely ancient porcelain bowl, held together only by its glaze. "Who hit me?"

"My friend."

"Some friend."

"He was waiting for us back here. He was going to help us get away. But when you freaked out he hit you. Then we couldn't get you to wake up, so we had to drag you in here before my parents got home."

"Who's your friend?"

She doesn't answer.

I turn to her. Her braid is undone but the weave of it still shapes her hair. Then I remember something else and pull the loose sleeves of her shirt down over her shoulders. The cut on her chest is a long deep scratch, made with the tip of a knife or a razor blade. It's still slick and shiny, not scabbed over yet.

"Did he do this to you? Your friend?"

"No." She shrugs the sleeves back up over her chest.

"Then who did?"

"No one."

There are voices in the hall. I feel her stiffen.

"Do they come in to say goodnight?"

143

"I'm fifteen," she says indignantly, but then amends that to: "Sometimes my mom comes in. Just to talk."

"What do you talk about?"

"How fucked up her life is, mostly. She gets drunk at night. My stepdad takes care of her. Listen, once they're in bed we got to go."

"Go where?"

"Away! We can take a bus. Then I could stay with you for a while. Get a job. I won't be much trouble. I promise."

"Are you crazy? I'd be arrested for kidnapping."

"They're going to arrest you anyway, remember?"

"For something I didn't do. That's different."

She sits up, very angry. She has changed so much just in the few days I've known her. That pale, unmarked face, now with a bump on her forehead where we crashed, the awful waterfall of dried blood down her chest, but worst of all the hostile bruised look in her eyes, as if she's been long acquainted with violence. Maybe the innocence was not there to begin with. Maybe it was in me, and the change I now see in me as well.

"You don't really care, do you?" she says.

"I do. But I can't leave here now. There are things I need to know."

"Like what?"

"Like who's your friend?"

"Nobody."

"Then who cut you?"

"Maybe you did," she suggests, taking my hand and guiding it under the loose shirt. "Did you ever think of that?"

144

My fingers brush against her soft tummy, sense the warmth of her breasts and linger there before she squashes them against the fresh tacky blood.

"No," I say. "I know what I've done and haven't done. I remember now."

"Well, then maybe it was your dad who cut me. I can say anything, can't I?"

"Pam, I want to help you."

"Just get out," she says. "If you won't take me with you then at least get out yourself."

"But I can't. Not while everyone thinks my father was . . . guilty of something."

"He was," she says simply, staring at me.

The light in the room has changed. We both sense it. The crack of yellow under the door is gone, the hall light has been turned off. There are footsteps.

"My mom," she says. "You've got to go. I'll get in trouble."

"What do you mean, my father was guilty? What did he do to you?"

"Go!"

She hustles me to the window, black bushes level with the sill. But I stop.

"In Melissa's room, those clothes in her drawer. Are they yours?"

"Of course they are," she whispers, opening the window frame as wide as it will go. Behind her someone is knocking.

"Pamela?" a woman's voice calls.

"I helped you," she reminds me. "Now go! Please!"

I drop over the edge as the door behind her opens.

spLit – LEVELs

Needles scratch me. I land in mulch, lie silently while she closes the window. It's too good a seal. I can only hear the buzz of voices, not their words. After a while I crawl free of the shrubbery and walk out to the road.

Night is just as bright as day in the suburbs, but with different kinds of illumination—lawn lamps, stark anti-burglar bulbs, neon cables strung high over intersections. I turn to the dark circle of asphalt at the end of the road. Valley Court, genteel name for a dead end. The cheap scenery of lawn-and-house breaks off abruptly at the woods, a looming absence just beyond the lit-up night. The last house has a large lawn ornament. It's an almost lifesize statue of a maiden, set well away from the lamp so it only appears in silhouette. It's the same one I thought I saw across the street from the house, my first night back, with long stiff hair, not flowing and supple like Pam's, but wires, thousands of diagonals all leading down from head to shoulder. In the flickering light created by wind and leaves it seems to move.

"Hello?" I ask tentatively, feeling foolish.

The statue takes a step, the blank face eying me, the hair still immobile, but the body moving along the lawn with the slow tension of an animal about to bolt.

"You've been watching me," I call, still unsure. "Do I know you?"

She disappears into the woods.

I stand frozen, not sure if what I'm seeing is real. The bump on the back of my head has grown. This circle of asphalt is so inexplicable. I look up to the sky and half expect to see an alien spacecraft, hovering.

Night can't hide the black sedan parked down the street.
A figure is slumped in front. It's Anderson of course,
staking out my house. I'm too far away for him to notice.
I cut across everyone's backyard, come up to Sally's and
peer around the corner. Occasionally he raises a cup of
coffee to his lips.

Her back door is locked. Ringing the bell, having Anderson see the lights go on, is too big a risk. A ladder is
lying by the side of the house. Slowly I step out, aware
I'm within his view if he looks in the car mirror. I pick it
up and carefully turn around. In back again, I prop it
silently against the shingles, right next to where the bedroom should be. The aluminum rungs shake, exaggerat-
ing the fear in my knees as I climb level with the window.

She is arranged in bed, just as she described, with
shiny satin sheets and the discreet smell of perfume. The
window is open a crack for air, but stuck.

"Sally," I whisper.

"Mmmm?"

Her eyes stay closed.

"Sally, it's Allen."

She props herself on one elbow and looks at the door.

"Over here."

"Are we eloping?" she asks, rubbing her eyes and looking down, then pulling at a sheet to cover herself. "Did I
forget?"

"Help me in."

"I can't. I'm naked."

"I've seen you naked."

"But not here," she points out. "This is my bedroom. Only Bob Bates, my husband, can see me naked here."

"I'll close my eyes."

"You better."

When I open them again she's in dowdy flannel pajamas, straining the window frame against swollen wood.

"It's the humidity," she says. "Should go down now that fall's coming."

I crawl most of the way in, then flop the last few feet onto the floor. She sits back on the bed and observes, doesn't take her eyes off me while reaching for a cigarette from the night table.

"You're tracking mud."

"I'm sorry."

"Oh, I wasn't thinking of the carpet. I meant that if they're following you—"

"They're not."

She shrugs, finally lowers her eyes as she tries getting a light.

"I only do this in moments of extreme stress," she explains, missing three times with the match. "What the hell are you doing here, Allen? That policeman is right outside, sitting in his car."

"I know."

"You know? Then you were a fool to come back, weren't you?"

"No place else to go." I sit up now, cross-legged on the carpet. "What about you, Sally? Have you been out tonight?"

"What's that supposed to mean?"

"Nothing."

I watch closely. She looks away, searching for an ash-tray, holding the cigarette at an angle.

"I don't keep one in the room," she excuses herself, getting up. "Have to use a dish from the kitchen."

My gaze stops her at the door.

"Don't worry. I'm not going to signal for help," she smiles. "I can take care of myself, remember?"

While she's away, I get up and go through the drawers of her dresser. The clothes are all severely ironed, like new. At the bottom, under everything, wrapped in plastic, is a small wafer-thin rectangle of steel, still crusted with blood.

"I brought you cake," she announces, coming back with dishes in both hands.

I hold up the razor blade. "Were you going to put this in my pocket, in case the handkerchief wasn't enough evidence?"

"No," she says. "I was going to get rid of it, when I had the chance."

"Where's it from?"

"Your sister's bedroom. Someone must've planted it. I found it the other day while those cops were there, when I was getting clothes out of the dresser. That's why I kicked that man. I thought he might spot it as I walked by."

"Why bother?"

"Because they don't allow conjugal visits at the federal penitentiary, that's why." She puts her hand up on the door frame and winks. "I still have high hopes for us, you know."

"Then you don't think I killed him?"

"I don't think you could kill five minutes in a whorehouse, Allen. Now eat, will you? I defrosted that myself."

I take the flowery china dish and silver fork. It's lemon cake, still hard as an ice cube. I lick a little to be polite.

"Know what they called me in the service?" she asks proudly, getting back into bed with her cigarette. "Suzie Homemaker."

"As a joke, right?"

She frowns. "What do you mean?"

"Nothing. You never answered my question. Have you been out tonight?"

She blows a jet of smoke across the room at me.

"Let me tell you a story, Allen. Back at the institution where I was raised, they called this one 'The Boy Who Would Not Inseminate His Neighbor.' Once upon a time, there was a very desperate young man whose butt was always being saved by other people, particularly women, particularly me. And the thing is, he'd never reciprocate. Instead of saying, 'Thank you'; or, 'Is there any way I could possibly repay you?'; or, 'Sally Bates, I love you and want to be the biological father of your child,' instead of saying anything like that, he would accuse them, go ransacking their rooms, and not eat the cake they had especially cut for him."

"What did you cut this with?" I ask. "A chisel?"

"That's not the point."

"I saw someone tonight. A woman."

"Well, good for you!" She's leaning forward, tendons

150

stuck out all around her neck. "I really don't want to hear about it."

"It wasn't you out there, watching me?"

She shakes her head, grinds the cigarette into the dish and puts it aside.

"Do you know who it was?" I ask.

"No."

"Sally—"

"I don't know, Allen."

I stare at her.

"I can't believe I'm having this conversation without a drink," she tells the ceiling.

"You were raised in an, an orphanage?"

"Huh?"

"You said, 'at the institution where I was raised.' "

"Oh, yes. I am the product of an unwanted pregnancy. Which, considering my present predicament, is kind of funny."

"Is that why you want to have a child?"

"I want to have a family!" she says fiercely. "I want to find out what being a mother is like, seeing as how I never had one myself. I want to make things right. Don't you know that feeling?"

"Of course I do."

"You got a funny way of acting on it." She looks down at herself, brushes some ash off her chest. "Am I ugly?"

"You're beautiful. But I just—"

"—rather fool around with that pathetic piece of jail-bait. Yeah, I recognized her at the funeral. I'm the only one that did, though. Don't worry. I didn't tell nobody nothing. You're just like your old man."

"No, I'm not."

"Longer you stay here, more like him you're going to get," she goes on.

"What's that supposed to mean?"

"You know. I heard all about him now. About him and your sister, I mean. How old is the girl, anyway? About the same age as Melissa was, right? Sixteen?"

"She'll *be* sixteen."

"Uh-huh."

"It's not true, the things they say about him. He loved Melissa, like a father loves a daughter, I mean. Like a father loves his only daughter. If anything, he was *too* protective. After, when my mother died, maybe he had some obsession, some private cult of missing her, imagining her, but nothing . . . nothing like what people say."

"But there's always a bit of truth in what people say, don't you think? Take me, for instance." She unbuttons her pajama top. "They probably say I'm a slut, which is one hundred percent wrong. But here we are in my bedroom, and it is my optimum fertilization time."

"What about Bob?"

"Bob won't be home till dawn."

"You love him?"

"Too much to talk about," she says. "He's my manchild. But that doesn't mean I don't have feelings for you too."

"What kind of feelings?"

"Pity, mostly. Pity and lust."

The walls of the house vibrate, shudder like a train is passing.

"What the hell was that?"

We both go to the window and see nothing. She leads me out front to an unfurnished room with bare wood floors. Light from the street jumps crazily here, magnifying flaws in the glass over the unadorned walls.

"The nursery," she explains.

A ball of fire has appeared in the middle of the road. There are no sirens in the background, no people coming out of their houses. It's all eerily quiet. It takes a moment, then we realize what's happened and go running down the stairs. By the time we get to Anderson's car, flames are roaring out the windows so high they meet over the roof and unite in a solid sheet.

"Look!" She points at the blown-out windshield. Anderson is still inside.

Without thinking, I take a step forward. The heat melts my features. I feel my mouth and eyes loosen, like they were made of plastic, dribble down my face. The dead smell of burning hair. Mine or his? I see just his hand, outstretched but limp. I pull it and try to leap back, feel its wedged-in tug of resistance. The rest of him is below the dashboard. There's a scream. Air escaping? Sally? Sirens? Finally, the dark bundle flows onto the ground, a badly packed duffel bag, everything shifting inside the cloth. Then someone pulls me away from the vortex of heat to where it's cold. The black asphalt of the street slams into my face. He hauls me up again. I expect to be hit. Instead, it's a figure out of a dream, Steven Wertz, dressed as he was for the funeral, holding me by both shoulders.

"Breathe!"

I exhale instead. Pure smoke. Cough until my lungs

crack. He sits me down on the curb and goes back for Anderson. Two fire trucks, both lime green, are foaming down the car. An ambulance has arrived too.

"Is he going to be all right?" I ask, a few minutes later.

"They think so."

"We saw it from the window," I say, trying to forestall his questions.

"We who?"

I look around. There's no Sally, just curious neighbors now, and even they mostly stand inside their doors looking out. But Sally's house is dark.

"How did you get here so fast?" I ask.

"It was my shift," he says. "We were taking turns."

"Watching my house?"

He looks past me, as if the split-level was responsible.

"Yeah. Harley knew you'd come back. By the way, you're under arrest."

"Holy shit." Gorgeous George stands before us in new jeans, without fringes or holes. To compensate, though, he wears no shirt. The red and white turret lights of the fire engines splash his ridged chest and narrow waist.

"Move it along, son," Wertz says.

"Mr. S, are you OK?"

"I'm fine, George."

"I wonder who it was?" he says to himself.

"Who?" Wertz asks. "You see something?"

"Yeah."

He scratches his head. I've never seen anyone actually do that before, scratch their head to think.

"I saw someone," he says. "Walking by the car. The guy inside started to get out, and then she threw something in. The whole street went up. Wow, you should have seen it."

"She?" Wertz stares at him.

"Yeah. Some girl."

"A kid, you mean?"

"I don't know. It was dark."

"Where were you?" I ask.

"Nowhere. Just going for a walk."

Wertz and I both look at his naked torso.

"I was hot," he says.

"You were going for a walk," Wertz summarizes. "At four A.M., without your shirt."

"Yeah. I couldn't sleep. I was thinking." He makes it sound like the first symptom of a fatal disease. "So I was just walking around and—"

"You know something?" Wertz looks him up and down. "You got goose bumps."

"Maybe I'm cold now." George stands his ground, shivers slightly.

Wertz takes out a piece of gum.

"And you smell," he finally says.

The boy frowns, makes an abortive motion to look at his underarms.

"Not there. Jesus!" Wertz trades me a look of commiseration, as if I was his partner. "I got a great sense of smell. Check it out."

I go over to George. He smiles a little too broadly. His skin is amazingly white.

"You're right," I discover, sniffing something over my own smoky clothes. A strong chemical odor.

George shifts nervously from foot to foot.

155

"Maybe gasoline," Wertz shrugs, getting up. "Huh? Maybe you spilled some gasoline on your shirt and then you threw it away."

"No," George says. Then his whole face collapses. "OK, I confess."

Wertz raises his eyebrows. His hand even strays to his waist, where his pistol is tucked in his belt.

"Confess to what?"

"I was out here."

"Watching the house?"

He shakes his head.

"No, I was . . . Come on, I'll show you."

He leads us past the burned-out car, four or five houses down, to a wide front yard of turf unbroken by trees or bushes.

"This is where Nina lives," he says, turning to me. "You remember Nina, don't you?"

"His girlfriend," I translate.

Wertz looks back over his shoulder.

"What the hell does that have to do with Harley getting torched?"

"I was here because he won't let me see her anymore."

"Who?"

"Mr. Rau. He says I can't go out with her because I'm older." Again he appeals to me. "I'm eighteen. I mean, can I help that?"

Wertz is sniffing again.

"It reeks here," he concludes. "Same as on you."

"There's my shirt." It's stuffed halfway down a sewer opening. "It has herbicide. I was pouring it on his lawn."

"Herbie Who?"

"Grasskiller," I say. "You poured grasskiller on her lawn, George?"

It's a beautiful one, expensive trucked-in sod rolled like a carpet. You can even see the green when it's dark out, the color is so true.

"It was to declare our love," he says, retrieving the can. "See, I drew a heart with our initials in it, hers and mine. So in a few days, when the grass turns brown, it'll spell out how much I care about her."

Wertz passes his hand over his forehead.

"You killed the guy's lawn?"

"Haven't you ever been in love?" he asks. "Anyhow, I parked far away so he wouldn't see me. I turned around to come back and that's when I saw this woman with long hair throw whatever it was into the car. The can of herbicide was still open and some was spilled on me. I was afraid that when you smelled it you might think . . ."

"We know you'd never do anything like that, George," I smile, and even pat his naked shoulder.

Wertz takes out his gun.

"All right, get down on the ground."

"Me?" I ask.

He looks confused for a moment. The pistol is trembling.

"No. Him."

"But—"

"He fucking murdered the guy's lawn! You know what it's worth, that sod? We're talking thousands." He dangles the cuffs with his free hand. "You step away from him."

"I'm not going anywhere," George assures him, getting down slowly on one knee.

"Shouldn't you be looking for the woman who tried to kill your partner?"

"Don't tell me how to do my job," he snaps, but does turn to George. "She have long hair? A long dress too?"

"I think," George answers. "Yeah, she did have a dress on."

"Shit." Wertz nods slowly, changing his mind, and tucks the pistol away. "I got to go."

"You know who it is, don't you?" I ask. "It's the woman I saw tonight. And you know who she is."

"I got to go now," he repeats.

"Wait," I call. "Aren't you going to arrest me?"

But he keeps walking, somewhere else already.

"Can I get up now?" George asks.

I shrug.

"Sure."

He brushes off his knee, looks soulfully at the thick lawn.

"It's like the way love is in my heart," he tries explaining. "It's there inside, spelling something, but you can't see it yet. It hasn't come out yet. But it will. Nothing can stop it. It's in— What do you call that? In-something."

"Inevitable."

"Yeah." He smiles, hugging himself in the cold. "It's inevitable."

"That's beautiful, George," I say, still staring after Wertz.

He jingles the keys to his car.

"Hey Mr. S, can I drop you someplace?"

"What if the world is just a big farm run by aliens who eat our brains?" Johnny proposes, pouring me another early morning screwdriver. "It would follow there are good and bad eras. Like cavemen. They probably tasted completely different than, say, the Greeks."

"This is your theory?" I ask, trying to follow, trying to stay perched on my bar stool too, dazed by the rows and rows of bottles.

"Well, your brain is shaped different depending on how evolved you are." This is obviously a rehearsed speech. He enumerates the points on his fingertips. "See, the cortex, that's the outside covering of the brain, it has more wrinkles the more complex a creature you are. So they probably taste different too."

"Have you ever had brain?"

"Not a human one, of course. I've had cow brains," he says modestly, looking down at his huge belly. "They're good in *beurre noir*. That's black butter. I had rabbit brains too, when I went hunting with my cousin. They're tiny. A rabbit's brain and his balls are the same size. That must be why they canoodle so much."

"Canoodle?"

"Cheers."

He lifts his glass. It's fizzy tonic he's made almost syrupy with vodka.

"So the cavemen," he resumes, "I see as tasting crude, just like a hunk of meat with a lot of gristle and fat. Now the Greeks, they're cleaner, more a classic cut, like sirloin."

"How does this help you, Johnny?"

"Well, it explains things. Death, for instance. When you die, you're just being harvested by some superior being, like fruit being picked. And what goes on around us, our whole lives, that's the feed they shovel into this pen to make our brains taste a certain way. What they're really eating is our experience of life."

"I can see why my father enjoyed talking to you."

"I enjoyed talking to him, too. He was a good man."

"Was he?"

"Of course he was." He wipes the counter.

"You know it's funny, I can barely see his face anymore."

"Not funny at all. That's perfectly normal. It's too soon. You have to forget before you can remember."

"You think I look like him?"

"Your dad? A bit." He glances at his watch. "Hell, I just realized here it is, Saturday morning, and do you know that you came in here the exact same time he used to? Isn't that something?"

"Something," I agree, unsure what.

Outside, it's still the same day, just with different lighting. Since I've spent the night awake, people now seem strangely round, like objects on rotating pedestals. I smile into my drink.

"Where is she, Johnny?"

"Where's who?"

His undershirt, visible across the Y of his collar, has black fingermarks, the kind you get from reading the newspaper.

"Is she in back?"

He frowns, still holding the wet rag.

"I'm sorry, but I don't know what you're talking about."

"This mystery girl. The one nobody wants me to know about. It's his day, isn't it? Like you said. He'd be here now. And so would she." I get up, sway slightly from all the drinks, but feel good, loose and instinctive. "You see, I've been following her all night without realizing it. In the Valley. In front of my house. And then it hit me, this is where she'd end up."

"Now who's been telling you stories?" he asks, not budging from behind the counter.

"Everyone," I say.

"Well, that's obvious." He sees me looking toward the purple curtain hung in the doorway leading to the back. "Go ahead, take a peek if you want. I don't know what you're expecting to find, but put your mind at ease."

He takes my glass and dumps out the ice. I push through the curtain and walk into a hallway packed high with boxes. The walls, when they do appear, have that old-fashioned two-tone paint job, sickly green at eye level, then dirty white above. Off to the side there's an incredibly filthy toilet, a stopped-up sink with a bar of Ivory soap floating in a slow whirlpool along with big balls of hair.

I feel my way further. I can sense the room has widened, but the window punched in the cinderblock rear wall is covered with cloth. Light glows around its edges and glints inside the bottles of hard liquor that line the shelves. The smell of perfume is strong in the dusty air. I recognize it from my schooldays, a brand all the

161

girls wore.

"Hello?" I call.

My eyes haven't adjusted enough to spot the bed at my feet. I trip and fall down into a shallow cot. Something rubbery shrieks against my palm.

"Sorry about the mess." Johnny's standing at the entrance. "I didn't tell you about the light switch, did I?"

Overhead a wide bank of fluorescent tubes begins flickering on, one remaining a dirty pink while the other two snap into deadly brilliance.

"That's Rosie," he nods.

I turn her over, a blow-up doll with long golden hair and bright red lips. The lips are an O and have a hole in them. She's dressed in a Spandex tube top and a short skirt. Her eyes are on rollers and move when her head tilts.

"Nobody wants a piece of this." He rubs his belly gently, as if it were something apart from him. "So I keep Rosie, for when it gets slow."

"But they told me—"

"Sometimes," he says, "I let people come back here. Business is just so bad these days. There's couples who have no other place to meet. But your dad?" He shakes his head. "I can't imagine who'd be telling you that. And I can't imagine you'd believe it, about a fine man like your father."

"You're the only person who thinks that," I mumble, twirling a strand of her plastic hair.

"Well, I'm the only person who knows."

"Knows what?"

"That he didn't do what they say."

162

"But how do you know for sure?"

"Because I was sleeping with your sister myself back then. Not him."

"You?"

"I was older than her, of course. But not by much. Just three or four years. And I wasn't this big." He smiles, sitting down opposite me so there's now three of us on the narrow cot. He caresses the doll's hip and sits her up. She is jointed all over, at the waist, the neck, the knees. "Used to meet her at the playground behind the old elementary school. They tore that place down, you know. Declining birth rate. There's just grass there now."

"You were sleeping with Melissa?" I say again, trying to keep my eyes open. I am overwhelmingly tired.

"I've given you something," he says. "Put it in your drink, I mean. Hope you don't mind. I figured you might go crazy if I told you while your head was clear. Now I'm going to say what I know and then I'm going to let you sleep. They're still looking for you, aren't they? Well, they won't find you here. Just lie back and listen."

"I've had . . . a night to drink," I panic, two thoughts cutting into each other. The room is beautiful, each bottle of whiskey glowing with a pinpoint of light.

"You probably think I'm some kind of pervert," he says, staring into Rosie's purple eyes rather than look at me. "But I'm not. I'm just lonely. I let people come back here. They do all sorts of things. I never ask any questions. But me, I've got no one. See, the only person I ever loved was your sister. And she's gone."

"Gone?" I watch the room slowly spin, have that sickening sense the earth is moving through space and that my drugged body is one notch behind, one second out of sync.

"I just wish I'd been more responsible. I was the older one, but when she told me she was pregnant, all I could think of was how to scrape up the money to take her in for an abortion. I just never realized what she was going through mentally."

"Melissa was pregnant?"

"That's why she left, you see. The problem was we never talked enough. We never had the time. We were always sneaking around. She'd never just let me pick her up. She said your dad wouldn't have approved. She was terrified of him finding out."

"He wouldn't have approved," I say. "She was so young."

"Not really. Some women mature faster than others. Your sister, she was more grown-up than me. I miss her every day of my life."

I struggle to sit but I'm too far gone.

"She left?"

"She sure did. The day I was going to take her in. I'd found out about some doctor. It was different then, you know. You had to go at night. I waited for her. Hours. But she never came. Next morning I heard she'd disappeared. I went looking for her everywhere. That's why I left town. I spent years trying to track her down. Hoping. Praying." He shrugs, puts his arm around the doll. "Finally I came back. I live with her memory. And with Rosie here."

"You knew. You knew the whole time it was a lie about my father!"

"Of course I did. But I couldn't very well tell him, could I? That I was the reason his daughter ran off? So I just tried to cheer him up whenever he came in. I like to think we became friends. I undercharged him. Always poured him doubles. Gave him a nice presentation decanter for Christmas."

"She's still alive? Still out there?"

"Maybe," he sighs, getting up. "I don't let myself think about that too much. Not anymore."

"But don't you see? She's the one who—"

"I'm calling it a day," he yawns. "I'll close up in front. The back door locks behind. In the meantime you sleep. Here." He adjusts the doll and lays her down beside me. I crack my forehead against her blank, ideally American face. Her eyes stare into me.

"Wait!"

"I don't want to talk about it anymore. See, you're the first person I've ever told. Makes me feel all empty inside, letting go of a secret like that after holding it to myself so long. You'll see."

"Will I?"

"You stay here with Rosie. She's clean. I wash her every day."

"Johnny," I call, flat on my back.

"She can do everything a real woman can," he promises.

A cloud of perfume envelopes me. The lights snap off.

165

chapter 7

IN SPRING, THE BASEMENT floods. Salt still stains the cement floor from where the tide last broke and rolled back. The window, flush with the ceiling, shows a patch of lawn frozen in moonlight, the blades perfectly trimmed and robbed of color. The washer is on. I watch the suds, the clothes tossing like some volcanic landscape being endlessly formed and destroyed.

"You leaving?" Anderson asks, nodding at the machine, my shirt and pants finally spinning to a rest.

"Why not?" I move them to the dryer. "I talked to a real estate agent. He said he could sell the place in a week. Doesn't need me here."

He isn't badly burnt, more scraped up than anything. But he regards his surroundings with an amazed stare, eyes bulging.

"You look like you can't believe it's all still here," I

smile. "Did you have a near-death experience?"

He frowns.

"Got my eyebrows singed off, is what happened. I'm told I owe you. Thanks."

We shake hands. He doesn't let go.

"And now you're arresting me."

"I should," he says. "Any other law enforcement officer would."

"Then why don't you?"

"Like I said, I owe you. Besides, new evidence has come to light."

"What new evidence?"

"We'll keep you informed."

"You don't think I did it anymore?"

"I don't know," he says frankly.

The stairs are raw wood. I can see underneath them, little crisscross supports to each step, the mark of a carpenter's pencil. There are no chairs here, it's just a dumping-off station, family debris and essential appliances: the hot-water heater, the washing machines. Anderson picks up objects at random, careful to put them back in their dust-outlined spots. I flatten both my palms on the warm enamelled top of the dryer and let its monotonous rhythm run through my body.

"Where'll you go after this?" he asks. "Back to the city?"

"Maybe."

He examines his reflection in a serving platter.

"Lord, I do look old." He tilts it to get more light. "I was reading those reports again today."

"What reports?"

168

"About your sister's disappearance. The FBI had your dad under surveillance for months afterward. Did you know that?"

"No."

"They were convinced he knew something. Never could prove it, though. All those trips he made, into the city, out by the reservoir, looking for her. I was wondering, why did he take you along?"

"For company, I suppose."

"Company! I wouldn't put my child through that."

"I didn't mind."

"Didn't you?"

"Then why do you think he took me?"

"Play-acting maybe. He probably figured he was being watched. That fits, doesn't it? He was childish, from what I can tell. Sounds like he was putting on a show."

"Why would he do that?"

"Guilt."

"Are you saying he knew where she was? That he was just pretending?"

"I'm saying he wasn't actually looking to find her. That he was just putting on an act. Maybe after a time he began to believe his own lies. That happens to all of us."

"That's crazy."

"Is it? How well did you really know your sister, Allen?"

"Not well at all," I answer, staring into space. "In my memory she's always on the verge of becoming a woman, trembling on the edge of it, and then she's gone. It's like to grow up here is to disappear."

Anderson is about to answer, then his face changes. He

holds up his hand. We both listen. A floorboard creaks above us.

"You expecting anyone?" he asks.

"No."

He takes out his gun, flicks it to motion me aside. The steps stop at the door to the basement.

"Who has the key?" he mouths.

"Everyone." I am tired of all this, and call out, as loud as I can: "Hello? I'm down here with Lieutenant Anderson from the police."

The steps resume briskly, clacking like a woman's high heels. Anderson has just enough time to shoot me a killing glance before dashing up the steps, his gun held rigidly above his forehead like a rhinoceros's horn.

"Damn!" he says, when we get to the top. "Listen!"

The front door is open. It's the sound of an engine starting. By the time we get outside, my father's car goes tearing backward out the driveway, turns, and accelerates down the road. I glimpse a woman's face through the driver's window.

"Melissa?" I ask.

I watch it as long as I can, the figure sitting upright at the wheel, diminishing, her hair fluttering in the dark.

"Come on!" Anderson calls, hustling me into his car.

"Don't you have a siren?"

"This is mine. The department didn't have another unmarked vehicle," he shouts, leaning on the horn as we approach each intersection. "Are you *sure* that was your sister?"

"Not sure," I answer, squinting far ahead. There's

nothing to see now, just the occasional bounce as she takes the car over a bump and flies. "But for a minute there . . ."

"I saw her too, last night," he says. "Hold on! Just before she threw that incendiary device into the car. General age is right, maybe the same looks. Hard to say, after nineteen years."

"It can't be," I repeat, the one certainty I've held to all this time.

"Why not?"

"Why would she come back now?"

"That's what I'd like to ask her. Look where she's going."

"The culvert."

He risks a look over, then returns to the road.

"I thought you never heard of that place."

There's no traffic after midnight. We barely keep her in sight. Anderson's knuckles show against the leather-coated steering wheel.

"What am I doing here?" I ask, looking out, the landscape reduced to a blindingly rapid code of light and dark.

"ID-ing her," he says. "If you can. I know it's hard after all these years, but . . ."

"Are you saying she's involved in my father's death?"

"I'm saying I have questions to ask her. Like why her initials were found on the ceiling above the bath."

"He put them there."

"Sure he did. Slashed his wrists and then stood on the lip of the tub, stretched all the way up without spilling a drop of blood anywhere else. Plus I got ten photos of the ceiling taken the day we found him. Not one of them shows a mark."

"It happened after?"

He nods, still intent on the road. The turn onto the county highway sends me crashing against him. His gun, in its holster, bruises my chest. I smell aftershave and hospital tape. He gives a little scream.

"Are you OK?"

"Ribs," he says simply. "Cracked one or two. But I'm fine. I'm all full of painkillers, with a big dose of speed on top."

"Go slower. She'll see us."

"She knows we're behind her."

She must, because she floors it, then tries coming to a sudden stop. Instead, the car skids and flips spectacularly, slamming into the trees, then rights itself, every window shattered.

"Now you know how I feel," Anderson sympathizes. "The woman is death on automobiles."

We pull up alongside. The door is open. There's no one.

"Stay here."

He draws his gun and goes crashing into the woods. I wait a minute, then follow, hear his heavy shoes blundering through the leaves off to the side somewhere and down.

"Melissa?"

The steep slope guides me to the water. I crouch, so I won't fall, and end up almost crawling to the edge of the

172

stream. At water's edge I look up at the sky. Here at last is the moon, no longer obscured by the low cover of trees or the high glare of street lights. The stream collects and channels it.

"Melissa!" I call again.

There's a single sound, a plop, like a pebble dropped down a well. As my eyes adjust I see the entire scene is wrapped around a black hole, the opening to the huge pipe from which the sewage flows. A couple is on the bank, rocking in a shared motion. My voice, my hushed calls of her name, must sound to them like passion.

"Who's that?" someone asks.

"No one," another voice mumbles, resuming.

"Melissa!"

Footsteps too fast, trying to stop, come skidding down the slope. Anderson, his one hand busy with his gun, can't grab on to any passing tree or cement and flops belly first into the water.

"Damn," he says quietly, and limps to his feet on an obviously sprained ankle.

Two more lovers laugh softly in the dark. Then a figure moves from the bushes by the shore. It's her, in a long dress and high heels, with wildly flowing hair.

"You!" Anderson calls. "Halt!"

She disappears into the sewage tunnel, bending her head, her heels clicking on the cement. I splash after her, with each stride stepping on the moon, then haul myself up into the black.

From inside the pipe, everything is beautifully focused. Anderson appears in a perfect circle, hobbling a few steps, barely able to walk, before coming to the opening. He holds on to the rim for support, peering after me.

"Allen, come back here!"

Up ahead, her footsteps echo in on themselves, echoes of echoes, along with the trail of her scent. It rides the stench, a subtle, refined odor.

"Allen, come back here! She's dangerous!"

His voice is further away, stuck at the entrance to the tunnel, just bits of it now, mixed with the splash of our feet, the sound of our breathing. Hers is fast and shallow, mine hoarse and deep. There is no light. I am suddenly terrified that the walls of the pipe are getting smaller, closing in on my shoulders and head. I poke out my hands, scrape them against the sides.

"Where are you?" I ask, stopping, gazing as hard as I can, trying to pierce the void, as if light could shine from my eyes, twin beams of it.

She stops, too. I can tell because there's no sound now, no footsteps.

"I want to talk," I say, and have it come back to me, "talk," a harsh echo. The stream makes it impossible to sit. I slump against the curved wall, unsure which way is back and which way is forward. Even up and down seem dubious here.

A figure detaches itself from the floor. Her pale blond hair possesses what little light trickles in on the water.

"Allen?" she asks.

"Melissa?"

"No," she says irritably. "Not Melissa."

She takes off her hair.

"Corky?"

"I wish you'd stop calling me that," he says. "Nobody else does anymore. You might start something."

He puts back the wig and carefully adjusts it, lowering it with both hands like a helmet. I reach out. His dress is silk. It ends below his ankles. His legs are shaved.

"Oh!" he sighs. "I knew you'd take liberties. In the dark, too. A girl can't trust anyone today."

"Corky."

"Stop calling me that. If you're going to call me anything, call me Janine."

"Janine?"

"Isn't that a nice name? That's why I wanted to be a doctor, you know. To change people. The operations they do now are incredibly crude." He holds out his hand. "Come on. We can walk together if we climb the walls just a little. And God knows you've made me climb the walls these past few days, Allen."

His dress swishes in the dark. The sides of the tunnel curve in, tilting us together so our shoulders rub.

"You've been here before?" I ask.

"Every Saturday night."

"The culvert's where you go . . . ?"

"It's a pickup scene," he says simply. "You saw how dark it was by the bank. Those high school kids don't know their ass from their elbow, not to mention other parts of the anatomy. Then I just slip away, after."

"And that's enough for you?"

"No," he admits. "I'm in love with someone really. But he's confused by my devotion. This is just my way of blowing off steam, you might say."

"What were you doing at my house tonight?"

"Coming to talk," he says. "To find out if you were OK. And I got all dressed up, too. I was going to take you here. Show you. How was I to know that big lumpy policeman would butt in ahead of me?"

"You tried to kill him last night!"

"That was supposed to be a smoke bomb," he protests. "I followed the directions. I have one of those chemistry sets, you know, like Mr. Science? I can turn water into wine. Make smoke. I'm very into transformations. I guess you can tell."

"But why?"

"To help you get away, of course. He was watching your house. I knew he was looking for you. And I also knew you were a big enough fool to come back here."

"But I don't understand."

"I loved you, Allen," he says. "Growing up. And you're such a sap. The way you let everyone play you. Somebody had to help you out."

"I thought you were Melissa."

"You live too much in the past. You never see what's right in front of you."

"Are we almost there yet?"

"Look."

Light shows on the cement, a broad slanting slab of it. I run, stumbling. Kids, who must play this far in, have left cave drawings on the wall. The smell of night air, sooty and rotting, polluted with exhaust, hits me like pure oxygen. I splash through a shallow, iridescent puddle of rainwater and oil.

"Not cut out for life in the suburbs anymore, are you?" Corky observes, standing at the entrance to the pipe

176

while I try hugging the open space, bathe my face in the glare of headlights.

"Where are we?"

"Just past the last development. Off the highway."

The hearse is tucked under a looming overpass. Cars move by on a ridge. Their progress is slow, an all-night funeral procession. Between us and them is a patch of absolute wasteland. Not a field, not a parking lot, just earth, stripped and levelled, then left to become mud. It's the methodical nature of the destruction that's so impressive.

"What's that?" I ask, pointing to the sky.

The stars are blotted out by the necklace of highway lights. Far beyond them, forming whatever horizon there might be, are enormous blinking numbers: 7 11 24.

"The date?" I ask, thinking of the portions my mother left in the freezer.

"It's not the date. It's the Seven-Eleven," he says, hiking up his dress. "Where have you *been* the last hundred years?"

"Away," I mumble, still staring.

"You'll have to excuse me. My clothes are in back."

I turn away while he changes out of the rear door of the hearse.

"I'm sorry I totalled your father's car, Allen," he calls, his voice muffled as he pulls something over his head. "But I can take you away from here now."

"In a hearse?"

"You did pay for door-to-door service."

"Everyone wants me to go away," I say, staring at the sign, on such high poles. It's monumental, like the over-

pass. As soon as you get outside these islands of civilization the scale goes wild, battling the surrounding im-
mensity. "But I'm hungry."

"You can eat anywhere."

I shake my head.

"That was Wertz's house you were in front of last
night, wasn't it, Corky?"

He stops changing, comes over with only one leg
through his pants.

"Don't you ever bring him into this. Steven's the best
thing that ever happened to me."

"But how can you be seeing one of the boys who at-
tacked you? God, they held you down and hacked off
your hair."

"That was a long time ago," he says furiously. "Steven
was just going along with the others. He's weak that way.
But he's really a wonderful man, once you get to know
him."

"He is?"

"Besides, that moment made me realize who I was," he
goes on. "It was all made clear to me. If they were calling
me a faggot, then that's what I must be. So in some crazy
way I'm even grateful to those boys. And now one of
them thinks I'm beautiful."

The sign winks, a man-made constellation.

"The 24 means open twenty-four hours, doesn't it?" I
ask, changing the subject. "But Seven-Eleven means
open from seven in the morning to eleven at night. So
how can a Seven-Eleven store be open twenty-four
hours?"

"It doesn't *mean* anything," he says wearily. "It's just there. That's the whole point."

"It means food, doesn't it? They must have food. You want to come?"

He still smells of perfume. In his eyes, the headlights of cars travel from one corner, across the curving globe of pupil, then down again to narrow and disappear.

"When you used to look at me like that," he says, "I would get so weak. My knees would hit each other. It was such a pure love. And you never knew. You were so incredibly naive."

"Thanks for watching over me, if that's what you've been doing."

"It's what I've been trying to do."

"You don't have to anymore, Corky."

I turn to the blinking numbers and keep my eyes on them, as if they might not come back each time, as if I am the one blinking, between each heartbeat, stumbling across the caked mud plain, loose rocks and dead roots underfoot.

"Allen!"

I stop. But it's only a cry. Lost love. Nothing comes after it. I don't turn. He doesn't call again.

An hour later I finally approach the store. A wide access road curves with agonizing slowness off the highway, then widens into a flat, perfectly poured field of blacktop with gas pumps at the center. The sign's huge twin poles dominate, its lights lost in the sky. A rope hangs off one with something hard at the end. It clangs against the brushed steel. The column is bigger around than both my hands. I hug it, and feel the accumulated cold go into my body.

"Looks like something you'd use in a lynching," Sally says.

She is standing by the pumps, her hand resting casually on the Unleaded trigger.

"It's a flagpole," I discover, catching the rope and tying it fast.

"That's right. They bought 'em cheap from a stadium. You do notice things, Allen. I'll give you credit for that."

"What about you? How did you know I was coming here?"

"Well, you don't exactly sneak up on people, do you? We've been watching you on the Interstate. Bob has a pair of infrared field glasses he swiped from the service."

It's dawn in one half the sky, still night in the other.

"What are you here for, Sally?"

"To stand by my man, of course. It's Bob's last night. School starts soon. Thought I'd keep him company. Come inside, why don't you? You're shivering."

"It is cold," I admit, still holding on to the pole.

"It's almost fall." She smiles. "You hang on to that anymore and you're going to get stuck."

An unseen plane tears a small hole in the horizon.

"I know what happened to my father now."

"Do you?"

"I've been putting it all together these last few days."

"I believe it." She comes out from under the gas pumps, her shoes making distinct scraping sounds. "Like

I said before, you're tricky, Allen. Come on inside. We'll get you some coffee."

That wakes my hunger again. Suddenly my legs are weak.

"Food," I remember. "Is there food in there?"

"All the comforts," she answers. "Can you walk?"

"I'm fine."

I hold her, noting the bloodied razor blade from her dresser drawer, now held casually in her other hand.

"Quit it!" she giggles. "What's gotten into you?"

"Nothing."

"Allen!"

My hands reach around her waist until they touch the steel, still wrapped in thick plastic.

"He'll see us," she whispers.

"It's dark."

"I told you, he has all this surveillance equipment."

We go around to the back of the store. It's blind concrete except for a steel door. The cattails begin here, the swamp they drained to make the highway.

"You always carry murder weapons around, Sally?"

"Don't need to," she answers, kissing me. "My hands are registered."

"Then what did you bring this for?"

"Well to chuck it, of course. Throw it in the swamp."

"Why? It's evidence."

She raises her eyebrows.

"I know it's evidence. That's why—"

"Keep it," I say. "Give it to the police."

"Suit yourself."

I put my hand on her neck, touch the soft curve of her shoulder. A bird starts up out of the cattails.

"You're cold," she says nervously.

"I was just showing Allen around." Sally sniffs as we walk into the store. "Smells like hell in here."

It's brightly lit, with aisles of puffy metallic bags and shiny refrigerator cases lining the walls.

"What you smell is burnt dust." Bob Bates is lying on the floor. It looks like we've caught him in the middle of a seizure. His small torso is all twisted, writhing to try and push his head closer to a strip of register tacked to the baseboard. "I turned on the heat for the first time. Now I can't get it off."

"Is there a thermostat?" I ask.

"It's broken."

He pushes himself off the floor. All his motions are abrupt, athletic, different stages of some lifelong calisthenic exercise. He slaps his body all over, cleaning himself. Finally the hands slap each other, making dry applause in the hot room.

"It is a little close," Sally observes. "Can't open the windows, huh?"

"They're just plate glass," he frowns, extending a now clean hand. "Hello, Allen. We've been expecting you."

"So I hear."

"I'll prop the door," she says, and hoists a bag of charcoal briquettes to lean against it.

"I heard you say you were hungry." He nods to a television monitor and speaker surveying the gas pumps. "We have a microwave here, all sorts of canned selec-

182

tions, Karmelkorn, and"—he disappears behind the counter to miraculously rise on the other side, suddenly tall—"a Slushpuppy machine."

"The microwave will be fine." I hold on to the counter, leaning crazily over to read the selections on the rack behind him. Bob has built a little wooden platform to make up for his handicap so he can appear above the Formica. "You have everything here, huh? Like a general store."

"If there was a complete breakdown of order, this would be an ideal command post."

"I never thought about it that way."

"Have you ever wondered," he asks, as I squint across the space, "why America isn't mentioned in the Bible?"

"Now, honey," Sally calls, returning after setting the charcoal against the door. "Don't go riding that hobbyhorse of yours all over poor Allen. I swear, as soon as you get up on an elevated structure of any kind you get that itch to preach."

"It's not an itch," he says with dignity. "It's a calling."

"Well, hold the phone. At least until after he picks out his meal. Which is it going to be, Allen?"

"Beef Bourguignon?" I ask, more in disbelief than out of hunger.

Bob takes the plastic container from the rack—another slides forward to fill the hole—and carefully reads the cooking instructions.

"You don't have a prosthetic heart, do you?"

"Jesus, hon! It's Allen from next door. He's a potent young man, still."

"I'm aware of that," he says, setting the timer and standing back. "I just don't trust these things, that's all."

spLit-LEVELs

The TV camera sweeps slightly, a gentle ocean rock, to take in both sides of the gas pumps, as well as the parking lot.

"I can adjust it," he says, noting my interest. He pushes a button.

The scene shifts, as if he's changed channels, and shows the approach to the store, the exit ramp from the highway.

"I was just telling Allen that was your specialty in the service," Sally yawns, reaching across the counter and taking a candy bar.

"Night maneuvers." He gazes, entranced, at the milky white and grainy black of the cheap picture. "That's where I met you, dearheart."

"Ain't it the truth?"

The container of Beef Bourguignon rotates on a tray, lit by a weak bulb. The microwave makes a blowing sound.

"Anyhow," Bob resumes, still staring at the blank strip of road, "don't you wonder why America isn't in the Bible? Israel is. Egypt is."

"Greece," Sally adds, licking her chocolaty finger.

"Greece is," he agrees, turning now, placing both hands on the register and leaning out over us, above the digital 0.00.

"Why isn't America in the Bible?" he shouts.

The microwave answers, mercifully, with a sharp *ding!* He frowns, not sure where he is, then opens the door and hands me the container along with a napkin and a plastic fork.

184

"How much?" I ask, pushing around the noodles appearing in the fatty brown sauce.

"On the house," Sally answers, holding up her half-eaten candy bar. "The job pays minimum wage plus all you can eat."

"I'll tell you why," Bob smiles, looking down on both of us. "Because this country is outside the realm of God. Jesus has yet to appear."

"And when he does . . . look out!" She unbuttons more of her shirt. "Damn, it's hot."

"That's why we're hoping for a boy," he says to me modestly.

"Because he might be Jesus?"

"Why not? The Lord works in mysterious ways."

"Honey, can't you call someone?" Sally asks.

"I already have."

"How many times did my father come here?"

They both look at me. I fish around for the one lump of stew meat in my Beef Bourguignon and chew it—fat, gristle, tendon—for hours it feels like, while they stare.

"Just the once," Sally says slowly.

"It happened here, didn't it?"

"I don't know what you mean."

"Whatever is was that convinced you about my father. You're the ones who started the rumors about him again, aren't you?"

"Rumors! They weren't rumors. It was her who came in first," Sally remembers.

"Pam came here?"

She nods, looking to the propped-open door. The gas

pumps ripple in the overheated air. "Her and that guy."

"What guy?"

"Dearheart," Bob cautions.

"You know. Her dad."

"Stepfather," Bob corrects.

"What happened?"

"Well, your dad was just outside. I could see him on the TV screen. He was watching them, all tense."

"We were both here," Bob explains. "Sally was keeping me company."

"Anyway," she goes on. "The girl made her stepdad stop so she could get a snack. But as soon as he was down by the Slushpuppy machine, she took off. Your dad's engine was still running. Next thing I knew, they were gone. It's like he snatched her away. Except that she was willing, I'll say that for him. Still, at his age . . ."

"Did you call the police?"

They trade a look, puzzled.

"He is the police, honey," Sally frowns. "That's the point. I thought you knew."

"Pam's father—I mean her stepfather—is a policeman?"

A car passes by the monitor, on the approach to the store. I take one last bite of the revolting food and put the container down.

"Did you tell him?" I ask. "Did you tell him what you saw? That it was my father out there with his daughter?"

"Stepdaughter," Bob corrects again.

The car pulls up in front of the store. Two men get out.

"We were just being good citizens," Sally drawls.

"Now I am by nature liberal-minded. But what that girl uses for clothes I would not even consider suitable as undergarments."

"She's lost," Bob says sympathetically. "You should try and save the lost."

"Oh I try," Sally answers, looking squarely at me.

I run.

Outside, the two men from the car come after me. One is Wertz. I avoid him, swinging wide. The other tackles me from behind. Tar and gasoline, the tastes of pavement, mix in my mouth with the blood pouring from my flattened nose. A knee pins my shoulders. I try wrenching free but Wertz grabs my hair. Light finds my exposed neck.

"Allen," he says. "Just the person I'm looking for. Now you stay still."

The other has gone inside. I can hear the sound of his shoes on the loose grit of the asphalt, my ear is so close to the ground.

"Not here," he calls as he comes back from the store. "Bring him around the side. They say there's a room we can use."

"Aw, do we have to?" Wertz whines.

"I've got some questions to ask him," the voice orders. "Besides, look what they found in there."

Wertz whistles and leans right over my ear.

"All right, champ," he spits. "Remember, I'm your friend in this situation. It's my buddy here who loses control sometimes."

They haul me to my feet. The other one steps back and flourishes it in front of me, the blood-encrusted razor of Sally's, unwrapped now. The blade glints, catching the pink sun. It's the thin, mustachioed man from the police laboratory. Forensic.

"Everything you know is a lie."

We are alone in the back room of the store. Forensic has bad breath. He kneels in front of me, his eyes shining. I notice threadbare patches in his mustache. Behind him are cases of beer, hundreds of them, stacked in columns from floor to ceiling as if they're holding up the place. We are near the freezer case. I can hear its hum.

"What's your real name?" I ask.

He rocks back on his heels, disappointed.

"I've just given you a Truth," he pouts, drawing out the razor again, making a slow pass before my eyes. My arms are bound behind my back by Wertz's cuffs, then looped around a hot pipe. I don't know where Wertz is. After they dragged me in here, he disappeared. "I just told you that everything you ever thought, everything you ever took for granted, is wrong. That the physical evidence of the world is a lie. And you want to know my name?"

"I already know what happened," I say.

"How could you know what happened? I made it all up. The blood on your handkerchief, the razor blade in the drawer. I even got her to make those anonymous phone calls to the police, after she suckered you to the culvert. I created this whole world you're living in. And you say you know what happened."

"You didn't kill my father," I say evenly.

The razor wavers, inches from my face.

"I killed him," he insists. "With this."

He lays it against my neck, where the pounding artery makes it bounce, chilly at first, then warm.

"You wish you'd killed him, don't you?" I nod. "Why? To kill the part of yourself that makes you terrorize your daughter?"

"Stepdaughter," he says, his grip tightening on the razor. It shakes.

"But he wasn't you. He wasn't like you at all. Those things they said about him were wrong. All he wanted to do was save her."

"He kidnapped her. People saw. Everyone here knew about him from before."

"He was unlucky. And he was weak. But he made his own life. He wasn't controlled by you or anyone else. He was helping her escape. And he might have done it too, if those morons out front hadn't recognized him because they were neighbors. Isn't that right?"

"What I do with my family is my own business. He got in my way. Like you."

Wertz returns with a cup of purple snow.

"Slushpuppy," he explains. "They want to know why we're not taking him down to the station."

He seems a bit puzzled himself.

"Because he hasn't confessed yet," Forensic answers, without looking up.

"Oh, we don't need a confession. We got all that evidence." His breath is a blast of synthetic grape and tobacco. "Hey Allen, I told you, he gets a little crazy sometimes. You should've seen him on the football field. Dirtiest player in the state. Totally psychotic. But we went undefeated that year."

"He's sick," I say.

"Yeah, I know. But what the hell, he's my brother-in-law."

"You're bleeding," Forensic says dully.

The sharp warmth, like that interior burn you get coming in from the cold, is spreading down my neck and welling in the socket of my shoulder.

"Hey, you're right," Wertz says, mystified.

Forensic has dropped the razor on the floor by my leg. My arms are still locked in place. I nuzzle my chin and feel it slide, slick and sticky at the same time, against wet clothing. The pipe, which must carry the heat, burns a second spine up my back.

"My father was innocent," I tell Wertz, licking my lips.

"Shut up," he says, making a Boy Scout salute with his fingers and poking it into my neck. "I got to find the pressure point. Cut off the bleeding. What the hell did you do, Dick?"

"She disobeyed me," Forensic says, watching us. "Do you know how hard it is to maintain authority these days? Kids are such punks."

"How did you get her back?" I ask.

"I decoyed the old man out of the house. I called him up, said he could either meet with me or get himself arrested. When I showed, she was alone. He'd made up the sweetest little bed for her, and let her buy all new things. They must have been planning it for a long time."

"So that's who George saw in the window, you and Pam."

"Jesus!" Wertz is not listening. He takes out a hand-

190

kerchief and tries spreading it over the whole wound. "You must've hit the artery."

I can see it now, soaking down my chest, the stain creeping, permeating the fabric. Its progress quickens with each heartbeat.

"And then I killed him," Forensic says, his eyes glazed over. "When he came back and found us."

Wertz stops. His hands are crimson. He looks from one of us to the other.

"Wait a minute," he says to Forensic, confused. "You told me his *dad* was the pervert."

"He's been playing you," I say, staring, trying to get across that I know his secret, about Corky, the fear he must have of exposure. "He knew just what buttons to push to get you to go along with him. He always has. Don't you see? You said it yourself. He's psychotic."

"All right," Wertz decides. "We got to get you to a hospital. Dick, move over."

"I killed him like this," Forensic insists.

He stands up and with surprising strength clubs both hands down on his brother-in-law's neck. Wertz falls. His dirty blond head hits the pipe before landing on my chest. The tiny handcuff key goes skittering off.

"But it doesn't matter anymore," Forensic says sadly. "Last night she told her mother everything. You know, all I ever wanted was a family. It took me so long to get one. And it wasn't even real. I had to make one out of all the scraps that were lying around. Someone else's wife, someone else's daughter. But I loved them. Now one cries all the time and the other won't speak to me. We can't even have meals together."

191

The key! I lunge toward it with my whole body.

"I guess families die like everything else," he goes on philosophically. "I was just trying to keep mine together a little longer, that's all."

"Let me go."

"Why?" he smiles. "You're just like me. I can tell. You'll just go somewhere and start up this mess all over again. I can't have that on my conscience."

He walks out the back door, into the swamp.

"Wait!" I scream.

The cattails quiver, recording his progress. Then they stop.

"Wertz?" I ask. "Are you OK?"

The head doesn't move. I try jogging him awake. A wad of purple gum, still with the imprint of his jaw, lies visible in his open mouth.

"Wake up, dammit."

I'm cold, despite the hot pipe against my back, despite the hot blood and my frantically beating heart. I wrench my wrists forward and feel them burn against the metal. Wertz's head lolls and stares at me.

"Get up!" I say.

"Get up," he agrees, still in a daze.

I struggle to my feet, knocking him aside, riding the loop of handcuffs up the pipe. My legs stagger. Then the pipe gives. It shifts. Above me, I see where the overheated metal fits into a seal. The connection is soft, from the smoking heat. I throw all my weight against it and watch the pipe move more, an inch this time, almost pop out.

"Steven!"

192

"Janine," he answers happily, concussed, curled up on the floor in the fetal position, his palms together in a childish pillow.

I try again to push the pipe but it won't move far enough. I'm too weak. I brace against the wall and force myself, step by step, to plunge forward. There's a horrible shriek of metal as my shoulders begin to come out of their sockets, a wide deep groan of space, then an explosion.

"See, the Karmelkorn machine was out of control," Sally explains.

"It burnt out the thermostat," Bob adds.

"So the building just kept getting hotter and hotter."

Anderson's head moves like at a tennis match.

"We were just trying to be good citizens."

"He had a badge."

"They both did."

"Naturally, when we saw Allen on the road we called the authorities."

The helicopter chops the morning sun into wedges, hovering overhead.

"Nothing," a bullhorn voice reports.

He makes a signal and it moves to land on the parking lot.

"You let two police officers," he shouts, either out of anger or because of the noise, "take a suspect into your storeroom and *torture him?*"

"What's wrong with that?" Sally shouts back indignantly. "Torture is part of life. If you knew what torture I go through every morning, just waking up in this God-forsaken place, knowing what I've done to myself and to other people, with a barren womb and sterile husband. If you knew what I dream at night—"

"My wife is high-strung," Bob apologizes. "This has all been a terrible misunderstanding. We thought that . . ." The helicopter is breaking up his words.

". . . Pervert . . . blood . . . time . . . police . . ."

"Don't worry, we'll find him eventually. He won't get far in that swamp," Anderson says, once they're stowed in the back of the squad car. "How's your neck?"

The bandage, with the brace over it, makes me feel like some newly born monster, stiff and unnaturally tall.

"Fine. I feel fine. They're not going to get in trouble, are they?"

He shakes his head, standing unsteadily on his bad ankle, then looks to the waiting helicopter.

"Borrowed it from the state troopers. Isn't she a beauty? I've got some business to attend to. Would you like to join me?"

"In that?"

"What's the matter?" he asks. "You afraid of heights?"

"No."

"Let's go for a ride."

We swing out over town. From up here it's revealed as still farmland, the lawns laid out like crops. Growing what, I wonder.

"Find your sister?" he asks casually.

"No." I shake my head, not bothering to yell. "It wasn't her, at the culvert."

"I know," Anderson smiles. "I traced where that sewage pipe comes out. Had casts made of the tire tracks. Not too many hearses in our area. Just the one, in fact."

"He was looking out for me. You won't—"

"A man's wardrobe is his own affair," Anderson answers mildly. "As for the rest, the department's going to take enough flak for having a child abuser on its force. Don't need to noise it around that one of our men was seeing a cross-dressing undertaker, too."

"Thanks."

"He will have to pay for my car, though."

Below us now, brown and lopsided, is George's heart of dead grass. It shows gamely against all the green. The initials he's tried to draw—his and Nina's—are wavy and uneven. Barely legible.

The helicopter bucks, rising higher and veering off. Sunshine shows all the scratches in the Plexiglas bubble. I shade my eyes and try following our progress. No matter where we head, though, it feels straight into the sun, which floods the space, warming only where it hits, but leaving the rest of the area ice cold.

"No atmosphere," Anderson explains, seeing me hug my arms, "this high up."

He motions to the pilot, who begins to take us down.

"You recognize this place?"

The rotor, as it slows, hisses through the air. I don't even try to answer until he takes my upper arm and pushes my head down, miming for me to follow him and duck under the lazily guillotining blades.

"In Saigon," he breathes, winded from the run, once we're safely past, "I saw a man's head come off clean from one of those things."

He gives the pilot a thumbs-up sign and the blades roar, spin into their own visual suggestion, beyond a blur, taking the chopper back up.

"Why did you send him away?"

"We're back in town. The Municipal Center. Don't you recognize this?"

I look around.

"It's where the old school used to be," he adds helpfully. "That's the back of the library. We're just behind it all."

The windows are mirrored glass. There are no doors. We are standing on a patch of packed earth, surrounded by lawn.

"And this was the playground." He spreads his arms. "I got out all the old maps. Don't you remember? You attended. I checked."

"Years ago," I admit. "But I don't see—"

He taps his shiny shoe against the earth. It rings, like a floor.

"Underground tanks," he explains. "This is where town's water supply is stored. It's piped in from the reservoir."

"So?"

"Ah, here she is. Been waiting for you, young lady."

Pam has come out of the library. She's dressed the same as when I first met her, an old woman's skirt, a white blouse that buttons up to her neck.

"I can't stay long." She faces Anderson, avoiding my eyes. "I'm on break."

"Just tell him what you told me," he says encouragingly.

"You know if everyone had just minded their own business this wouldn't have happened," she snaps.

"He was trying to help," I say. "How did my father find you in the first place?"

"I don't know. He was hanging around the library, I guess. Staring out that window on the second floor, right where I shelve."

"Up there." Anderson points, as if its placement has some great significance.

"We started talking. He said he had a daughter my age. He told me about the book he was taking out, how it was the history of this war that went on forever. I liked him. He was my friend. I don't know how he found out about Richard. I didn't tell him."

"He must have sensed it somehow," Anderson says. "Then followed you."

"Richard? Your father?" I ask.

"Stepfather. God, can't anyone get that straight? There's a big difference."

"How long had he been hurting you?"

"About two years."

"Didn't you want to get away from him?"

"Of course I did! That's all I ever wanted to do was get away. Your dad was going to help me. We had it all set. I'd already gotten new clothes. He was going to find me a place to live. Some town where I could go to school." She hangs her head, remembering.

"But why that night, right in front of Richard? Why not during the day when he was gone?"

"I freaked," she says. "It was just like any other time. We were going to that ditch. He liked doing it there. But when I saw your dad following us, keeping an eye on me, I just couldn't wait anymore. I ran to him. He understood. He was so happy I came to him."

"Then why did you let Richard take you away again that night? After he'd come to the house?"

"He said if I didn't, he'd do things to my mom." She looks up. "I'm sorry, Allen. I know I shouldn't have. But I was so scared."

"The man had been our forensics expert for some time," Anderson says. "Naturally I had no idea—"

"But you came back," I interrupt, keeping my eyes on her.

She nods.

"Later that night, I snuck out. I wanted to explain to your dad how I couldn't leave Richard now, ever, because of what he'd said he would do. I let myself in with the key behind the mailbox. That's when I found him."

"Where?"

"In the tub. He'd already . . ."

"He was dead?"

"Yes."

"About those bruises." Anderson hesitates. "I talked to the coroner again. Apparently they could have been caused by each hand holding down the other. In turn. To stop himself from shaking."

"His own hands," I say.

"Yes."

"He killed himself."

"I'm afraid so."

"I took the razor blade," she says. "I don't know why. It just looked so ugly, lying there. Then Richard found out—"

"And he cut you. Why?"

"That was later, to stop me from telling you things. To stop me from helping you."

"But the writing on the ceiling. The blood. You said it was someone else's."

"Richard did that," Pam answers. "He remembered about your sister. When you started hanging around and asking questions, that's when he had me steal your handkerchief and make those phone calls."

"He manufactured that evidence hoping you'd panic." Anderson says. "Panic and run."

"That's why he had me help you get away from the funeral. He said you'd just leave here after that. Then I thought I could get you to take me along, like your dad was going to do. But Richard was hiding in the house. When he heard you start asking me those questions . . ."

"He hit me."

"Yes."

"It was suicide, Allen," Anderson assures me. "Apparently the man wasn't a killer. Just sick."

"Then what am I doing here?"

"I think you know." He turns to Pam. "Tell us again what Allen's dad said to you about Melissa."

"He said she was still here," Pam mutters, almost inaudibly. "In the library, he told me. He said he could come here and be with her anytime."

"With her memory," I interpret.

Anderson laughs.

"No, brother. Here." He stamps his foot down again. It's hollow. He stoops, trying not to get his suit dirty, and excavates a big rusty ring. "Old access cover, for taking measurements. Before gauges. They must've used a dip-

199

stick."

He tries to lift it. It's like he's trying to pull up the lid of the earth. He shakes his head and groans, straightening again.

"Not as easy as nineteen years ago, is it, Allen? It's rusted shut now."

"I don't know what you're talking about."

"Sure you do. Doesn't matter, though. Wouldn't even be bones in there by now, what with fluoridation and all. That's what the County Engineer says. She's long gone."

"You mean she's in the water?" Pam asks.

"In the water, in the grass, in the trees. All around by now. In the guts of half the town population."

"Gross!"

"We were out looking for her," I say, numb.

"And you found her, didn't you? That night. What was she doing?"

"She was waiting for someone. He hadn't come yet."

"Who?"

I shake my head.

"Did your father hit her? Knock her down?"

"No! She saw him and ran. She fell. She hit her head on that ring. It was an accident. A terrible accident."

"Ah." Anderson kicks it. "And where were you?"

"In the car. Looking out the window. Like always. He told me to wait. But I could see. And then when it happened, I just sat there. I couldn't move. I kept watching."

"So you saw."

"I saw everything. He tried to make her come back to life. He breathed in her mouth. At first I thought he was . . . kissing her. But she stayed so limp. Then he pounded

200

her chest. He was crying. I still didn't understand."

"And then he panicked, didn't he?"

"He lifted the top of the tank and let her slide in. I couldn't believe what I was seeing. I was only ten."

"Did you talk about it?"

"No. When he got back to the car, he didn't say a word. We drove around more, for hours, pretending to look. But he must have known I had seen. We never talked about it."

"Ever? You never talked about it with *anyone*?"

"Of course not. When I got older and realized what had happened, by then all those rumors about him had started. I couldn't say anything. Think of how it would have looked. After all, it was an accident. And he was paying for it every day of his life. I knew. That was enough."

"Still, there's a difference between knowing and telling," Anderson says.

"It was like a dream. All of the past just came back to me in pieces. But I didn't want to put them together. I'd just see them over and over again. In isolation. They were just bits of something that didn't fit."

I look at Pam.

"He must have stayed here hoping for another chance, to do it right this time, to save a girl who was in trouble. And when he came back to the house and realized you'd gone, that he'd lost you again . . ."

"Stop," she says in a tiny voice. "I just wish everyone would . . . leave me alone."

"What's important is you finally told someone what Richard was doing to you."

"I did it for your dad. He's the only person I ever cared

about."

"Not for me?"

"You? Richard *made* me kiss you. You're old." She turns to Anderson. "Can I go now?"

"I got to go myself," he sighs. "All this translates into a year of paperwork, let me tell you."

"What about me?" I ask, still standing, staring at the ring in the ground.

"It's over," he says. "The investigation, I mean. Don't you feel better?"

"Better? Why should I feel better?"

"Because you're free to go."

I bend down and grasp the sun-warmed ring. But it's rusted shut.

"Don't even try," Anderson calls, watching me.

But I can't help it. I pull, and pull, and pull, until they are both long gone.

"Mr. S," a voice says. "Be careful. You're going to give yourself a rupture."

George is standing with his arm around Nina. He wears his mirrored driving shades. She holds an over-sized paperback, hugging it to her chest with both hands.

"You've been to the library?" I ask, trying to hide my surprise.

"We had to get a book." He nods to Nina, who opens the pages at random and displays a map of America.

"A road atlas?"

"They got all fifty states," he says admiringly.

"We're running away," she explains. "My dad—"

"Nina's going to have a baby." He looks to me. "I figure I got a car, so what the hell?"

"What the hell?" I agree.

"That fat guy who drove me at the funeral, I started telling him all about it. I don't know why. He said that no matter what we decide, we should get out of here first. I figure I'll worry about money later."

"Money's not a problem," I say. "We'll have plenty of money once the house sells."

"We? You mean you want to come too?"

"For a while. If you don't mind."

He looks down to Nina. She shrugs and even manages to smile.

"George likes you," she says.

"I like George. I like you both."

"Well come on, then."

We walk across the huge lawn.

"You feeling OK?" George asks, putting his arm around Nina. "Where do you want to go first?"

"Hawaii," she says.

"You two sit together." I go to the other side of the car. "I'll drive."

The road forms in front of us, it comes into being the instant we arrive. We're happening. We're gone.